HIS EYES HELD AN EXPRESSION SHE COULDN'T FATHOM. . . .

His mouth brushed softly against hers in a slow, lazy rhythm. Her eyes closed involuntarily, her body still rigid from the newness of intimacy with him, her lips faintly stiff as he traced them with his own.

His hands moved to her back, soothing, softly caressing, while his hard mouth gently parted her lips and moved between them with a firm but controlled pressure.

"Relax, Abby," he whispered, his voice deeply amused. "I'm only kissing you."

A LOVING ARRANGEMENT

Diana Blayne

A CANDLELIGHT ECSTASY ROMANCE™

Published by
Dell Publishing Co., Inc.
1 Dag Hammarskjold Plaza
New York, New York 10017

ISBN 0-440-15026-4

Printed in the United States of America
First printing—January 1983

To Our Readers:

We have been delighted with your enthusiastic response to Candlelight Ecstasy Romances™, and we thank you for the interest you have shown in this exciting series.

In the upcoming months we will continue to present the distinctive sensuous love stories you have come to expect only from Ecstasy. We look forward to bringing you many more books from your favorite authors and also the very finest work from new authors of contemporary romantic fiction.

As always, we are striving to present the unique, absorbing love stories that you enjoy most—books that are more than ordinary romance.

Your suggestions and comments are always welcome. Please write to us at the address below.

Sincerely,

The Editors
Candlelight Romances
1 Dag Hammarskjold Plaza
New York, New York 10017

CHAPTER ONE

The rain had been fierce, and Abby Summer dripped puddles into the rich carpet at her desk as she eased out of her beige trenchcoat and removed the jaunty little brimmed hat from her braided coil of silvery hair. Even wet, she had a grace and elegance about her that caught and held the eye. She was twenty-six, but looked years younger with her slender build, her delicate features.

The fingers that slid her wet coat onto a hanger were long and the nails expertly manicured. There wasn't a hair out of place on her head, or a smudge on her high cheekbones that wasn't deliberate. Her dark green eyes were as cool, as calm, as the face she presented to the world. Abby was notorious around the law offices of McCallum, Doppler, Hedelwhite and Smith for her serenity in the face of impossible odds. In the year she'd been Greyson McCallum's executive secretary, she'd never fainted, shouted back, burst into tears, or resigned. That, in itself, was a mark of heroism. Greyson McCallum had his own reputation, and serenity was certainly not part of it.

McCallum and old Mr. Doppler were the senior partners in the firm. Dick Hedelwhite was long dead, but his name was left out of respect, and Jerry Smith's just had been added. Abby and Jan Dickinson shared the secretarial duties, but Abby got the lion's share because of McCallum's larger clientele. He was nationally famous as a trial lawyer, attracting clients from as far away as New York, while Doppler and Smith specialized in divorce cases and civil suits. Besides, Jan had the advantage of working for two patient men. Nobody, ever, would have described McCallum as patient.

Abby uncovered her electric typewriter and reached in her middle drawer for the daily appointment book. When it didn't peer up at her, she blinked in amazement. It was always in the middle drawer.

She searched through the side drawer and found it tucked on top of a box of carbon paper where it had no business being. Odd, she didn't remember placing it there Friday at quitting time.

Her fingers opened the pages to Monday and she quickly scanned the familiar names and times until a heavy black scrawl stood out against the neatness of her crisp handwriting. McCallum had written in a name of his own for 4 P.M. and Abby felt the blood leave her face in a frantic rush.

Her hands trembled, dropping the black-bound appointment book on the glassy surface of her desk. Her eyes had widened at the name, and she felt a surge of panic that made her want to run out of the office. Robert C. Dalton, 4 P.M., Robert C. Dalton, 4 P.M.—the words ran around wildly in her mind.

Of course, it wasn't impossible that Atlanta could have produced a Robert C. Dalton. The phone book must have held at least a score of them. But Abby had a hunted sensation, and she'd have bet a week's salary that this particular Robert C. Dalton hailed from Charleston, that he was married to the heiress of a shipping empire, and that unless she found a way to be out of the office by 4 P.M. she was going to be drawing her unemployment by quitting time.

She'd been so interested in that name that she hadn't heard the intercom the first time it buzzed. The second sharp, impatient jab caught her attention, and she depressed the button with trembling fingers.

"Yes, sir?" she managed weakly.

"Bring your pad," a deep, curt voice replied.

She automatically reached for her steno pad and a pencil, dropping it once before she got to her feet. It was court week, and McCallum had a case set for 9:30 A.M. in superior court. It was just barely 9:00 A.M. now. It would take him ten minutes to get to the courthouse—five, the way he drove his sleek Porsche

—and he'd just found something he wanted to add to a petition. By the time he dictated it, she'd have less than five minutes to type it, with copies, in the spotless manner he demanded. And she knew before she tapped at the door and went in that she'd never be able to manage it in her present, shaken state.

"Sit down," McCallum growled without lifting his dark, leonine face from the transcript his eyes were glued to.

Abby sat, poised gracefully on the edge of one of the brown leather chairs, her eyes lingering on his broad shoulders, the big, square-tipped fingers that were gripping the transcript. He looked more like a professional wrestler than a famous trial lawyer. And it wasn't only his tall, powerful physique that commanded attention. He could use words more effectively than any weapon. Abby had seen him reduce grown men to tears on the witness stand. He could literally strip the hide off a stubborn witness without ever raising his deep, velvety voice.

No doubt, he curbed those aggressive instincts when he was with women, because the office always seemed to be full of them. Sophisticated, very mature women who looked vaguely alike, merging into one specific type: tall, brunette, generously endowed, and faintly bored. The zombies, Abby called them when she needed a mental boost. And their conversation always seemed to center around their newest perfume or McCallum's most recent gift. They all fawned on him. And none of them had ever lasted longer than a few weeks. At forty, he was still very much a bachelor, and in no evident hurry to change his status.

"Studying me?" he asked curtly, and his strange pale gray eyes suddenly caught hers in a hammerlock.

She fought back a snappy answer, barely maintaining her cool, efficient image. Abby kept her vibrant personality under tight wraps, disguising it in clothes like the plain gray suit she was wearing, the glasses she didn't need. She'd landed the job that way. Don't come on like a career woman, or a hothouse flower, her friend Jan had warned her when she applied for the job. Only McCallum's women were allowed to be colorful and vivacious. He only wanted an efficient wallflower at his typewriter, someone restful. So Abby had toned down her clothes and her personality, forgotten the outgoing charm that had made her a successful reporter, and walked right into the job. And she almost never missed the old life, the excitement. Almost never.

"Was I staring, Mr. McCallum?" she asked with a polite smile.

His eyes narrowed, and he watched her in that way he had, a piercing stare that seemed to reach deep inside to all the secret places that were locked away from the light.

Without replying, he neatly removed a sheet of yellow legal paper from the pad in front of him and slid it across the desk.

"Type that," he said curtly. "Then call Miss Nichols at her apartment and tell her I'll pick her up at seven tomorrow night for the ballet."

Without me, Greyson McCallum, you'd never be able to keep a love affair going, she mused silently. It was up to Abby to send them flowers and candy, run interference, soothe them when he broke dates, put them off gently when he was busy . . . it was almost as exciting as writing a gossip column.

"Yes, sir," she said, jotting down the note in the margin of her steno pad.

"Call my brother and tell him to cancel his flight to Paris," he added darkly. "He is not, repeat *not,* following that French prostitute home. And call my mother and tell her I'm heading him off."

More dirty work, she sighed, making another note. Nick wasn't going to like that. He was genuinely infatuated with Collette, and whether or not she deserved McCallum's careless appellation was up for grabs. Mandy McCallum wasn't going to be thrilled by the news, either—she doted on her youngest son, but she wasn't up to her eldest's temper. She muttered a lot, carefully making her remarks when Grey was out of earshot.

"And you don't approve of that, do you?" he asked suddenly.

She jumped at the suddenness of the remark. "Why . . . I . . ."

"Don't give me that sweet, vague little smile," he growled. "I can read you like the cover of a glossy magazine, Miss Summer. But I don't require your approval, merely your cooperation."

And my blind obedience, yes, sir, she thought, hiding the mutinous twinkle in her green eyes.

"He is twenty-five," she reminded him.

"Twenty-five, eh? And since when has a man's age had anything at all to do with responsibility when a woman like that is concerned?" He leaned back in his massive chair, lifting his hands behind his shaggy mane of hair. The action stretched his tailored white shirt over his broad chest, its sheerness hinting sensuously at the heavy, thick mat of black hair over those powerful muscles. "Hell, Miss Summers, you can't know much about men if you consider that brother of mine responsible."

That aggressive masculinity disturbed Abby. She distrusted it. He'd never made a bona fide pass at her, although she sometimes felt that it had crossed his mind. She deliberately made herself as unnoticeable as possible. McCallum was the kind of man no sane woman would risk her heart on. He was too arrogant, too independent, and too fond of variety. A brief affair was as much as he had to offer, and Abby had no faith at all in her ability to weather that type of arrangement. Despite a brief, unhappy marriage, she was still remarkably inhibited for a woman of her age, something of an anachronism in the modern world. She'd had her fingers burnt badly, and she was wary of enticing flames.

"I said, do you think Nick is responsible?" he

repeated, surging forward in the chair to rest his elbows on the desk, while his glittering eyes studied her from under his jutting brow. "What the hell is wrong with you this morning?"

She looked away from him and down at her pad. Well, she thought, it was tell him or make a run for it. "There's an appointment on your calendar for today that I didn't make," she said quietly, hoping against hope that it could be explained away, that it was a useless fear.

"Well, my God, do I need your permission to make an appointment on my own?" he demanded with a black glance.

"Oh, no, I didn't mean that," she said quickly. She hunched her shoulders helplessly. "I meant . . . Mr. McCallum, is Mr. Dalton . . . I know it's none of my business, but is Robert Dalton from Charleston?"

A strange expression passed over his face. One eye narrowed ominously. "Yes, Bob Dalton is from Charleston. Why? Do you know him? From where?"

She should have known better. She could have pumped old Mr. Doppler later if she'd kept her head, and he was so fuzzy minded, he wouldn't have asked for a reason. But McCallum was asking, and he meant to have an answer. She read it in his taut face as he watched her down his arrogant nose.

"It's nine ten," she reminded him. "You have a client waiting . . ."

"He can damned well wait, or the judge can postpone the arraignment, or Jerry Smith can handle it for me, but you're not leaving this office until I get an answer." He took a cigarette out of his shirt pocket and lit it, dragging the big ashtray toward him. He leaned back again. "Well?"

"It's none of . . ."

"I hired you," he reminded her. "And not without reservations. If you think that disguise you wear has fooled me, you're crazy. You're shook up today, Miss Summer. As shaken as I've ever seen you, and unless I miss my guess, Bob Dalton is the reason. Care to tell me about it, Abby, or shall I call Dalton and ask him?"

"Is he a friend of yours?" she asked weakly.

"In a manner of speaking," he nodded. One silvery eye narrowed. "Come on, woman, talk."

She lifted her face proudly, hating the betraying tremor of her lower lip. "His wife found him on the bed with me," she said steadily, watching the surprise lift his heavy brows. "She had me fired from my job, and I left Charleston . . . because of the mess."

He stared at her levelly for several seconds before he spoke. "When?"

"Over a year ago," she said evenly. "I was the assistant news editor on an afternoon daily at the time."

There was a long pause before he suddenly picked up the receiver and punched a number out. A minute later he was telling his junior partner to take the case for him, and giving instructions.

"You can pick up the brief here, and get the lead out, boy, you've only got fifteen minutes!" He slammed the receiver down.

He stared at her silently for several seconds, taking a long draw from the cigarette before he spoke.

"Were you in love with him?" he asked.

She shrugged. "I thought I was, yes. I could have died when his wife opened that door. She went white in the face and began to scream obscenities . . ." Her eyes closed on the terrible memory.

"What did Dalton do?"

The question stung, because it brought back the humiliation full force. "He told her that I'd seduced him," she replied with a bitter little smile. "His wife had the moneyed background, you see. A divorce would have cost him everything, and I wasn't worth that. So I left Charleston and he kept his empire."

"You knew that he was married?" he asked, and she saw a glint in his eyes that she couldn't identify.

"Yes, I knew." She laughed mirthlessly. "Strangely enough, it didn't matter. I loved him too much to care. And we'd spoken often enough about his loveless marriage, his plans to get a divorce. I wanted to believe him. I hadn't learned that it's dangerous to want anything too much."

"How do you feel about him now?" he asked quietly.

She met his eyes with an effort. "I don't know. I haven't seen him since it happened. And I don't want to. I'm afraid," she admitted in a whisper. Afraid that I'm not over him, that he'll smile at me and make excuses, and I'll believe them because I want to believe them, her thoughts ran on. "I haven't even dated anyone since I left Charleston."

"I know," he replied, and something in the way he said it puzzled her. "You needn't look so puzzled, Miss Summer, I read people very well. You've worn a suit of armor since the day you walked into my office. It's very effective."

"I didn't want to get involved with anyone," she said, wanting him to understand. It was suddenly important to make him understand, not only that she was afraid of Dalton, but why—because she'd never given herself to him completely. His wife had barged in just in the nick of time. But McCallum's eyes had gone past her to the door.

"Come in, Jerry," he said, motioning his tall, fair-haired partner into the office. "Here," he said, handing him the brief and tacking on a flurry of instructions.

"Don't worry, boss," Jerry grinned, winking at Abby. "I've been well taught. I'll murder 'em!"

"I don't have time to defend you, so don't go past contempt of court," McCallum said dryly.

"You bet. See you!" And he was gone with a wave.

McCallum swept his piercing gaze back to Abby. "What do you want to do? I don't have time to break in a new secretary with my present calendar," he added menacingly, "so don't mention resigning. It'll take three weeks night and day to train a new girl, and I can't spare the time. I'm not that easy to please."

"If you weren't so impatient . . ." she began.

"Damn it, don't start trying to make me over," he shot back. "I'm too set in my ways. I don't want a teen-ager who'll get hysterical every time I lose my temper, and I can't take simpering spinsters. It took me long enough to get you over bouts of crying in the ladies' lounge."

She glared at him. "It was only once, and you threw a book at me!"

"The hell I did!" he growled, sitting up straight. "It sailed off the desk into your lap, but I didn't throw it. It slipped."

"You have a nasty temper, Mr. McCallum, and I'd hate to sacrifice some poor young girl to replace me, but I can't stay here if you and Bob Dalton are going to be working together for any length of time."

"I'm taking him on as a business partner," he said, confirming her worst fears. "And you're not quitting me. So just calm down and we'll work something out."

"What did you have in mind, your worship, hiding me in your closet when he comes to town?" she asked sarcastically.

One thick eyebrow went up, and there was faint amusement in his silver eyes. "Your mask slipped."

"Don't think it's been easy keeping it on around you . . . sir," she replied.

"Then why bother in the first place?" he asked impatiently.

"Because Jan said you wanted someone efficient, cool, and unflappable," she replied coolly.

One corner of his chiseled, hard mouth turned up and his eyes were suddenly speculative. "Well, well. Now you're making me curious, Miss Summer."

"About what?" she muttered.

"About what you're like under that facade. I think I'm going to have to find out."

"You won't have time," she assured him, getting to her feet. "If Bob Dalton is coming here at four, I'm leaving permanently at three. I've had my life turned upside down once, I'll just pass on this round. There are other jobs."

"Like what—reporting?" he challenged.

She swallowed. "It left a bad taste in my mouth for a while, but, yes, I think I could go back to it now."

"Running?" he taunted.

"Exercising the better part of valor," she corrected, firing up at his mocking smile.

"I thought you were interested in writing novels," he remarked.

She flushed. "So?" she challenged.

"So don't throw away your new life without a fight," he said, rising from his own chair to tower over her.

"I can't stay!" she cried, her eyes wild, her face flushed.

"Of course, you can," he corrected, moving closer. He looked down at her with dancing eyes. "All you have to do is move in with me."

CHAPTER TWO

She stared at his solemn face blankly while she tried to decide whether or not she'd misunderstood him.

"You heard me," he said, reading the question in her eyes. "If you're obviously living with me, he won't dare make a pass at you. He wants this deal between us to work out too much to risk it, even for you."

That was true enough. McCallum's size alone was enough of a deterrent. And he was blatantly possessive about his acquisitions, especially his female ones.

"Do you think I have to actually move in?" She tried to sound her usual cool and reasonable self, but she could hear her voice faltering just a bit. "Couldn't we just appear to be having a very *obvious* affair?"

He sat back down in his chair, eyeing her in that totally unnerving way of his. "Certainly a possibility," he replied. "But tell me, Miss Summer, if Bob Dalton turned up on your doorstep late one lonely night, would you be able to keep him on the other side of that door?"

She stared back at him for a long moment, then down at her hands clasped in her lap. She gave no reply to his question, and he seemed to acknowledge that none was necessary.

"But Mr. Doppler and Jerry . . . and your mother and brother, what would they think?" she countered to his silence. "Everyone would know!"

"It would hardly be effective if we kept it a secret," he reminded her with a dry smile. He stuck his hands in his pockets. "If you're worried about sex, you needn't be," he said bluntly. "You must have noticed by now that my tastes run to brunettes who don't interfere with my work. You won't have to lock me out of your bed."

The blush was unexpected, and it seemed to fascinate him. A faint smile touched his lips.

"Well?" he asked. "This is the twentieth century, honey," he reminded her gently. "People are living together all over the city. And you aren't still in pigtails."

That hurt, but she wasn't going to waste her breath trying to explain her feeling about such things to him. Twentieth century or not. It didn't seem to matter to him anyway. He was so matter-of-fact about it, as nonchalant as if he asked women to live with him every day. She studied him quietly. Perhaps he did. And he was offering her his protection, without any risk of involvement. It would keep Bob away from her, of that she was sure. Robert Dalton's cowardice had surfaced once during their brief relationship and she did not flatter herself into thinking for one instant that he would risk losing this deal with McCallum for her sake.

Besides, she told herself, her parents wouldn't have to know and Grey's family would understand, she hoped. She couldn't bear to have them think less of her for it. Their opinion mattered. Grey's opinion mattered, and she'd only just realized it. She stared at him helplessly, wanting to put it into words that she couldn't seem to find.

"How long would I have to live with you?" she asked practically, after a minute.

"Two weeks," he replied. "Dalton will be in town that long while we discuss business—and he's going to visit friends in Dunwoody. After that, it won't matter anymore and you can move back into your own apartment."

"When do I have to pack?" she asked.

"This morning, obviously," he replied with a curt laugh. "He's having dinner with me tonight. Mrs. McDougal is cooking seafood for us."

"Oh." She couldn't imagine how she was going to get everything packed by late afternoon. And she couldn't imagine, either, how she'd let herself be talked into this. No wonder McCallum had such a reputation for charming judges and juries. She didn't know what had hit her, and she'd seen it coming!

He turned and hit the intercom switch. "George," he told Mr. Doppler, "Abby and I are going to be out for the rest of the morning. If I have any calls, have Jan take them, will you? Thanks."

He flicked off the switch and the next thing Abby knew, she was being put into her raincoat and hat and herded out the door.

It felt strange, having Greyson McCallum in her apartment. He'd been there before, to give her a lift to work once when her car was in the shop, or to deliver a sheaf of scribbling that he needed typed on Saturday. But having him sit on her dark brown sofa sipping a cup of coffee, with his pale eyes watching her narrowly while she darted around getting books and essentials packed, was disturbing. He made the small efficiency apartment seem even smaller.

"I'm still not sure I'm doing the right thing," she said a few minutes later, with her suitcase packed and sitting on the rug by her floral upholstered easy chair while she shared a last cup of coffee with him.

"Afraid of what people will say?" he chided.

She flushed, the rosy color complementing her creamy complexion and lighting her wan face. "Yes, a little. I've always been pretty conventional. I don't know if I'm going to like having people stare at me like a kept woman."

"Haven't you learned by now that people can only hurt you if you let them?" he asked with a cocked eyebrow. "Who the hell cares what people think?"

She stared down into her fragrant coffee. "You forget I've been there before," she reminded him. "And I've got the scars to prove it."

He crossed his long legs and stared at her over the rim of the cup. "How old are you?"

"Twenty-six," she said without thinking.

"You look like a twenty-year-old, trying to impersonate my maiden aunt in that outfit," he laughed softly. "I hope you aren't planning to wear it tonight?"

She bristled. It was an expensive suit. "What's wrong with it?"

"It isn't the kind of outfit a sophisticated woman wears," he said matter-of-factly. "You'll have Dalton questioning my eyesight. And I presume you didn't dress like that for him?"

Damn his bluntness! Her small chin lifted proudly. "I won't disgrace you," she said sharply.

"Don't bristle," he admonished. "Do you need those glasses?"

With a self-conscious grimace, she took them off and folded them, placing them on the table beside her.

"Or to screw up your hair in that ridiculous bun you always wear?"

With an exaggerated sigh, she took out the hairpins and let her long, silver hair flow around her shoulders. The effect was stunning. He watched her with a steady, narrow gaze that made her want to lock a door between them. He'd never looked at her in quite that way before, and she wasn't sure how to take it.

"Tell me about Dalton. How did it begin?" he asked.

She drew in a deep breath. "There isn't a lot to tell. He was running for office, for city commission, and I interviewed him. He was easy to talk to, very charming. He invited me to tour his shipyards, I went, and we started seeing each other. It was just an occasional cup of coffee at first, and then one day . . ." She shifted restlessly, remembering the feel of the tall, blond man's arms around her, the stunned expression on his face that first time he'd kissed her, the feel of his hard, expert mouth on hers. . . .

"Stop daydreaming and finish it!" McCallum said curtly.

She dragged her mind back to the present. "He said he loved me," she replied, skipping over the rest. "I believed him, perhaps because I wanted to so much." Her eyes dropped as she remembered Dalton's silky voice pleading with his fiery wife, denying his own part in it, assuring his wife that Abby had tempted him one time too many. . . .

"Was it worth it?" he asked with a bite in his voice, and her temper ruffled. Not for worlds would she have told him the truth then, that it had never gone the last mile between Dalton and herself.

She glared at him.

"How long did you stay around after his wife caught you?" he asked.

"Two days. It was either run or be run out of town. Dalton's wife comes from a family with plenty of pull. So, I ran. Atlanta was home," she explained. "I grew up with Jan," she added. "She said I might be able to work for you, since your secretary was leaving to get married. But she said I'd have to blend in with the woodwork."

"So you became a chair," he mused. "I see. And didn't you miss chasing ambulances, Miss Summer?"

"Not after the first month," she confessed, glancing at him with a shy smile. "You have some of the most incredible people around you. There's always something going on where you are."

"The next best thing to the police beat?" he asked.

"Or the social page," she murmured, grinning. "Your love life is one big, ongoing adventure . . ."

"Don't bring love into it, honey," he corrected with a half smile. "That's a word I'm not used to."

She shrugged. "Whatever. Working for you is never dull."

He scowled at her. "You look different without your disguise."

Her hands made a helpless little gesture. "I don't suppose you were fooled from the first, were you?"

"No, but I was curious." He lit a cigarette and blew out a cloud of smoke. "I wondered why a girl with your intelligence would be working as a secretary. And why you went to such lengths to hide your beauty and avoided every pass my brother made at you." He chuckled at her blush. "At first I thought you might have undergone some trauma in adolescence. You wore an invisible 'don't touch' sign. But you were efficient, and dependable, and I kept you on despite my initial doubts. You were very restful," he added with a grin.

He got to his feet, staring down at her intently. "No turning back," he warned softly. "If you commit yourself this far, you're going the whole way. Walk one step toward Dalton and you'll rue the day you met me."

She believed him. That raw power in him was more obvious now that she'd seen it in a personal way. She knew how ruthless he could be, and she didn't want to have that wall fall on her.

"I won't back out," she promised. Her eyes searched his narrow ones. "Why are you doing this for me?"

He smiled mockingly. "I don't want to lose the best secretary I've ever had."

"Oh."

"I hope you packed an evening dress," he added.

She smiled, thinking of the sexy little black dress in her suitcase. "Oh, I think you'll approve, even though you don't like blondes."

"You'd better thank your stars that I don't," he replied in his deep, gravelly voice as he went to open the door with her suitcase in his big hand. "Otherwise, you might be jumping out of the frying pan and into the fire."

"What is Mrs. McDougal going to think?" she asked, frowning.

"Will you stop?" he growled. "For all I care, she and the whole bunch can think we're madly in love and too inflamed by passion to stay off each other."

"They'll know better," she stammered.

He lifted an arrogant eyebrow at her. "Then we'll just have to let them find us making love on the couch, won't we?"

She'd never thought of him that way. But the pictures that flashed suddenly into her mind were graphic and embarrassing. To lie in those big, powerful arms and let his mouth crush down against hers. To feel the hunger in it and taste it, to feel his skin under her hands . . .

She followed him out the door in a stunned silence. She hadn't counted on being curious about him, physically. That changed things, and she wasn't sure in what way.

His apartment was like the man himself—big, sophisticated, elegant, and imposing with flagrant contrasts at every turn. The furniture was antique—genuine; she was sure. The rugs were Oriental, the statuary was modern, marble pieces mostly. There was a plush gray sofa around a fireplace, down in the sunken living room.

"Where shall I put my things?" she asked hesitantly.

He led her down the hallway and opened a door into what was obviously the guest bedroom, with a deep blue decor that was pleasant and restful. He set her suitcase and overnight bag inside the door.

"This is yours for the duration," he said with a hint of humor in his tone. "But for the sake of appearances, when Dalton's here and you need to freshen up, use the master bedroom, not this one."

"All right. But . . . where is it?" she faltered.

He led her to the room across the hall and opened the door on a dark curved oak bedroom suite with a huge, king-size bed overlaid by a silky chocolate quilted coverlet, flanked by heavy tables with broad-based lamps.

"No comment?" he asked, studying her averted face. "Not even on the size of the bed?"

She gave him a sneaking glance. "There's a lot of you," she agreed.

He laughed softly. "And I'd look strange in a canopied French Provincial bed," he added.

She couldn't stifle a laugh at just the thought of it. And then she remembered something and the laughter vanished. "Will Mrs. McDougal be in today?" she wondered aloud.

"Probably," he said. "Don't worry so. She's not a busybody. She never interferes."

But all the same, it wasn't going to be pleasant, having that very kind woman giving her curious looks. She'd known Mrs. McDougal for several months. She respected her, and she didn't want the plump housekeeper to think less of her. It was a crazy idea, anyway, and God only knew what effect it would have on McCallum's private life. Speaking of which. . . .

The phone interrupted her thoughts. McCallum answered it, and Abby went into the living room to give him some privacy. But it was a brief conversation, because barely two minutes later, he joined her.

"That was Jan," he murmured. "Dalton won't be here until Wednesday." He glanced at her and smiled. "It's just as well. I wondered how we were going to break the news to the staff and make it believable."

She felt the relief all the way down to her toes. Two more days. In that length of time, a lot could happen. The world could end. . . .

Her green eyes darted up to his. "What about Vinnie Nichols?" she asked. "Will you tell her the truth?"

"I might as well take out an ad in the Sunday magazine section of the newspaper," he replied gruffly. "My God, you know what a gossip Vinnie is."

"But . . ." she faltered.

"We tell nobody the truth, Abby," he said curtly, his eyes level and silver. "Unless you'd rather back out?"

The alternatives were all unpleasant. There'd been

enough change in her life in the past few years. She was weary of flight, of trying to outrun problems. She liked her job, she liked her life the way it was now. She shook her head slowly. "No, Mr. McCallum, I don't want to back out."

He lifted an eyebrow at her. "How many people are going to believe that you can still call me Mr. McCallum when you're supposed to be sleeping with me?" he asked.

She shifted uncomfortably. "I'm sorry, but old habits die hard. I've never called you by name, even behind your back." She studied him. "Although," she admitted dryly, "I've called you a lot of other names behind your back."

"No doubt." He smiled faintly. "Mother calls me Greyson. Nick calls me Grey. Vinnie calls me Cal. Take your pick. But no more 'Mr.' Fair enough?"

"I'll do my best," she promised.

He took her to a quiet little cafe around the corner and she had a club sandwich and a cup of coffee while he acquainted her with the routine of his apartment. She knew that breakfast was at six sharp, that he liked peace and quiet, and he didn't care for hose hanging in the shower.

"Oh, aye, aye, sir, I'll be sure to leave my collection of aboriginal fertility rite recordings at my old apartment," she assured him.

"Twenty-six, did you say?" he asked mockingly.

Now she was finishing the first half of her sandwich and watching him over her coffee cup. He was bigger close up than he seemed to be in the office, broader and darker and much more imposing.

"You're staring again," he remarked without looking at her as he poured cream into his coffee.

She shifted. "Would you rather I stared at the man behind you?"

He chuckled softly. His silver eyes pinned her. "How have you managed to be so sedate while you were taking dictation all these months, Miss Summer?" he asked. "Surely you had to bite through your tongue a few times."

"More than a few." She sipped her coffee, feeling awkward without her coiffure and glasses. Her whole outlook was different now, with the facade taken away, as if age had fallen away with the bobby pins. "But I liked my work, and I didn't want to be fired." She glanced at him impishly. "I needed to blend in with the woodwork, you see."

"Jan exaggerates at times," he reminded her. "I did want an efficient secretary, but the role of an aging spinster hardly suits you." His eyes narrowed, studying her. "Didn't you tell me once that you were divorced?"

She didn't like even the memory of her marriage, but she nodded.

"How long ago?"

"Three years."

"Children?"

She shook her head stiffly.

Her fingers tightened on the cup. "Are there any more personal questions you'd like to ask me before we go back to the office?"

"Only one," he replied, not even ruffled by her rudeness. "Was Dalton involved emotionally?"

"He never told me. I think he was . . ." She studied the floor. "I was lonely and he was kind. Perhaps I was blinded by my own feelings."

"How long did the affair last before his wife caught you?" he asked casually.

"Ah, that's the irony of it all," she said with a bitter smile. "We'd only just realized that we were going to have an affair. Fortunately, she walked in while I still had some of my clothes on."

He set his cup down with deliberate slowness and stared at her across the table with narrowed, studious eyes. "In other words, he hasn't had you."

"Shades of the Spanish Inquisition!" she burst out.

"Is that how I sounded?" He finished his coffee. "I suppose I'm so used to the interrogation room and the courtroom that I tend to forget how to carry on normal conversations."

"What *are* you going to tell Miss Nichols?"

"Have you called her about the ballet?" he asked.

"But we rushed out of the office, and I didn't get time . . ."

"I'll talk to her this afternoon." He leaned back in the chair. "I'm going to tell her that we're having an affair."

"But she'll be so upset . . ." she protested, remembering how fragile-looking the small woman was. Abby liked her, despite the fact that she dyed her hair red and tended to put on airs.

"I'll console her with a diamond bracelet," he said carelessly. "She won't miss me."

She glanced down at the shiny surface of the table. "Is it always that easy for you to let go of people?"

"I love my freedom, Abby. I like a woman I can take or leave, hadn't you noticed?" he added with a raised eyebrow.

"It's very hard to miss a parade," she agreed. "They don't last very long."

"I wear them out," he remarked with a slow, sensuous smile.

Sex was little more than an unpleasant memory for Abby, whose husband had expected everything and given nothing. It had been a part of her marriage that she tolerated, but never really enjoyed. Even with Robert Dalton, her caresses had been a way to please him, to repay him for his kindness. More enjoyable perhaps, but never thrilling. She'd never felt touched to her very soul, never out of control. She had the feeling that she was a little cold, a little frigid. She'd never wanted a man with the kind of raging passion she read about in her endless romance novels. It had often surprised her that she found those same love scenes so easy to write.

"Deep in thought, Abby?" he asked. "Don't you think I'd be a good lover?"

Her surprised gaze met his head-on. "I'd never thought about it."

"Ouch." He lit a cigarette with a wry smile on his face.

"No offense," she said quickly.

"None taken." He studied her face with a scrutiny that was just a little short of embarrassing. "Will you think about it now?" he asked with the bluntness that was characteristic.

She averted her face. "Shouldn't we get back?"

He stood up and paused to leave a tip under his saucer. He didn't say another word, but she had an odd feeling that she'd given him the answer he wanted just the same.

Two clients came and went before McCallum called Abby in for dictation.

After he got through the pile of letters that required answers, he watched her for a long time, his eyes going from the loosened, waving platinum hair, down the soft lines of her body to the sleek legs encased in smooth hose peeking out of her skirt.

"Now *you're* staring," she observed.

"You've got nice legs, Miss Summer," he murmured, and his narrowed eyes slid over them like caressing hands.

She laughed, her whole face lighting up at the unexpected compliment. "Thank you."

He grinned back at her. "My pleasure. Well, Abby, is it going to be today?" he asked, leaning back in his huge, padded chair to study her. The action pulled his shirt taut across the broad, hard muscles of his chest, and her eyes involuntarily went to it, curious about the sight of it, the feel of it. Her own thoughts were faintly shocking and she looked away.

"Today?" she echoed, only half hearing him.

"You do realize that if we're going to make Dalton believe we're having an affair, the office staff is going to have to believe it as well?" he asked quietly.

"Yes, of course." She stared at him, waiting.

"Do you think telling them would be enough?" he taunted.

He pressed the intercom button to get Jan. "See if George has that Burlough file, honey, I'd like to look through it."

"Yes, sir," came the pleasant reply.

McCallum's silver eyes caught Abby's and held them, while something prodded her heart, causing it to beat wildly. Her breath caught.

"Open the door a little, Abby," he said in a deep, slow tone that was as rich as velvet.

Like an automaton, she laid down her pad and went to open the door a couple of feet.

"Now, come here," he added softly.

She went around the desk, but hesitated at his side, looking down at all that vibrant masculinity, the darkness of his hair, the uncompromising lines of his face. She was surprised to find herself a little afraid of him, a little shy.

He reached out and caught her around the waist,

pulling her down onto his lap with a short laugh at her involuntary gasp.

Her eyes stared into his from a distance of inches. Her cheek pressed against the fine fabric of his suit jacket. She could hear the regular, strong beat of his heart under her ear. He smelled of expensive cologne, and his face was immaculately clean shaven, his mouth chiseled and firm and wide.

"That's right, look at me," he murmured deeply. "You never have."

Her lips parted on a shaky sigh. Her fingers laid nervously on his white shirt, and under it she could feel warm flesh and the springiness of chest hair and it made her pulse tremble with new sensations.

One big finger traced a sensuous line around her full lips, teasing them, tantalizing them. "I've wondered if that pretty mouth was as soft as it looked," he murmured before he bent his head to find out. She looked up into darkening eyes with an expression she couldn't fathom as his mouth brushed softly against hers in a slow, lazy rhythm. Her eyes closed involuntarily, her body still rigid from the newness of intimacy with him, her lips faintly stiff as he traced them with his own.

His hands moved to her back, soothing, softly caressing while his hard mouth gently parted her lips and moved between them with a firm, but controlled pressure.

"Relax, Abby," he whispered, his voice deeply amused. "I'm only kissing you."

It didn't feel like only a kiss, though. There was a world of experience in that expert, taunting mouth, in the hands that knew so well where to touch, how to touch. She was aware of his hard-muscled, powerful thighs under her, his massive chest against her. She felt as nervous as a schoolgirl with him, and it was unexpected to find that she liked the way he was kissing her.

"Stop holding yourself away from me," he whispered against her mouth. "It's like making love to a virgin. Give in, Abby; stop fighting me."

"I'm trying," she whispered. "Grey, it's been a long time . . ."

"This isn't going to convince anyone," he growled. "But maybe reason is less effective than this . . ."

He took her mouth roughly, and she felt his tongue darting into it, taking possession, while his massive arms swallowed her against him. She couldn't even fight, it was too devastating. This was a lover's kiss, and even Dalton's hadn't been so sensuous.

Desire welled up in her slender body as his tongue thrust slowly, deeply into her mouth with a demanding pressure that made her body curl into his. He lifted her even closer, one hand in her hair, the other sliding down to her spine to urge her flat stomach against his in a new, urgent intimacy.

She gasped under his ardent mouth, her hands flat against his chest. She could feel the warmth of it, the steely muscles under the spring of curling hair. She wanted to open the buttons. She wanted to touch him, to press her face against his warm skin, to hold him against every trembling inch of her body.

There was a sound outside the office door that barely penetrated her whirling mind, followed by a faint gasp and the sound of footsteps retreating quickly. Abby was only aware of it on some subconscious level until McCallum lifted his head, glanced toward the doorway, and smiled mockingly.

"Discovery," he murmured, glancing down at Abby. He was as calm as if he'd been fishing. His pulse was regular and slow, his breathing normal, not a hair mussed. Abby's heart was punishing her, and she could barely breathe. She couldn't believe he'd weathered that stormy interlude without any effect, but perhaps it was only an appetizer to him.

"Jan, unless I miss my guess," he said, gazing at her flushed face, parted lips, and wildly disordered hair. "A little cooperation on your part would have been welcomed, but I think she got the picture just the same."

"I . . . I did cooperate," she murmured, puzzled.

"Did you?" He studied her quietly.

Abby brushed a strand of hair away from her misty eyes and sat up on his hard thighs. "Well, I learned one thing," she said, with a little of her irrepressible humor returning as she glanced at him. "I learned why there's a parade through here."

He chuckled softly. His narrow eyes studied her for a minute. "Just for the record," he asked as she struggled to her feet and moved demurely away from him, "how long has it been since a man kissed you?"

She gave him her haughtiest smile while he drew up an ashtray and lit a cigarette. "Nick did, as a matter-of-fact, at the Christmas party. Very nicely, too. Which reminds me, are you really determined to make him stop seeing Collette?"

He glared at her. "My private life, and my family's, is none of your concern, Miss Summer. Don't you have some letters to type?"

The sudden change from lover to autocratic employer hit her like jet lag. She hesitated just an instant before she retrieved her pad from his desk and walked back into the outer office, closing the door without looking back at him. In the months that she'd been his secretary, he'd never spoken so coldly to her before.

Jan cornered her in the ladies' room during break, her eyes wide and openly curious.

"Busy?" she asked.

"He's got a full calendar." Abby could just barely meet her friend's dark eyes. She hated the deception already. "The White case comes up next week, you know, in criminal court."

"Do I remember," Jan groaned. "I had to help you make phone calls and set up appointments and type petitions . . . at least we got paid for all that overtime. Can you imagine the D. A.'s face," she added with a mischievous grin, "when he sees all those exhibits

McCallum's taking into court? Not to mention the surprise witness."

"It will be war," Abby agreed, grimacing. "And, as usual, he'll call up here and want to grind Mr. McCallum into grits, and guess who'll get to soothe him?"

"I'll take you out to the new lobster place that day," Jan promised.

"You're a nice person," Abby told the short brunette.

Jan glanced at her and away. "Uh, Abby, I . . . well, there was a file Mr. McCallum asked me to bring in a few minutes ago."

Abby was busy trying to repair the damage McCallum had done to her mouth and hair. "And?" she asked, forcing herself not to blurt out the whole painful story.

"He was kissing you," came the soft reply. "Whew! was he kissing you!" the smaller woman added with rolling eyes.

And hadn't felt it at all, Abby could have told her, but why that should be disturbing puzzled her. "He . . . he asked me to move in with him," she blurted out, waiting tautly for the reaction.

"With McCallum? You're going to live with McCallum?" Her friend sat down in one of the two chairs and sighed. "I should be so lucky. What about that bottled redhead?"

"I don't know," she replied quietly. "He said he'd tell her good-bye with a diamond bracelet."

"I'd rather have McCallum," Jan giggled. "Wouldn't you?"

"What a question!" She ran a small brush through her glorious tangle of platinum hair.

"It's just like that novel of yours you let me read the first few chapters of," came the wistful reply. "You know, where the business executive falls in love with his secretary and has to take her away from his best friend?"

Abby put her brush back into her purse with a sigh. "But there's no married and living happily ever after in it," she said. "Or with McCallum, either."

"Once he gets to know you, who knows?" Jan asked softly. "Far as I know he's never lived with anyone before."

If only she could tell Jan the truth. She hated the lies, but when she thought about Robert Dalton, she knew there was no other way.

In her mind, she could still see him. Tall, blond, slightly graying—a sophisticated man with a kind of tenderness she'd never experienced. It had been the tenderness more than anything else that had attracted her. Life hadn't been gentle with Abby. The very newness of being treated like procelain had undermined all her nervous defenses.

McCallum hadn't been tender, she recalled suddenly. She could remember vividly the hard crush of his mouth, the leashed strength in his big body as he'd held her so intimately. She'd never realized just how experienced he was. How could she, when he'd never touched her. Even at the Christmas party, she'd been afraid to let McCallum catch her under the mistletoe. Although, honestly, he hadn't even bothered and that had stung. So had his remark about her lack of "cooperation" in his office a few minutes ago. She hadn't fought him. She flushed. She hadn't kissed him back, either. A small part of her was afraid to wake the sleeping lion in that vibrant body, for fear of what it might cause. And she didn't take time to explore that nagging curiosity, either.

"How about some coffee?" Jan asked as they went back out into the carpeted reception area where their desks were spaced widely apart. "I just made a fresh pot."

"I'd love it. Maybe I'll have time to finish the scene I was working on last night while we have our break."

"Abby, honestly, do you ever do anything except write?" came the exasperated reply, followed by a gasp and a giggle. "What a silly question. Sorry!"

Still smiling, Abby sat down at her desk and pulled out the long yellow legal pad that contained her scribbled notes. McCallum and Jerry and even old Mr. Doppler teased her about her writing ambitions. Everyone knew that it was her dream to become a novelist. She ate, slept, and breathed it, a habit that even went back to the old days in journalism. Writing was what kept her going, the one thing that gave her loneliness dignity, that made life bearable. It was more than an ambition. It was husband and child.

She scanned the page, a torrid love scene that led her two main characters into a fiery argument—the old ploy of getting them together while keeping them skillfully apart until the end of the book.

"Abby, what do you want in your coffee?" Jan called.

"Oh, I'll fix it." Abby jumped up, leaving the legal pad on her desk to join her friend in the office's compact conference room. The coffee smelled delicious, its rich aroma meeting her at the door.

"Aren't we lucky?" she sighed, taking her cup gratefully from the small brunette. "Our very own coffeepot."

"Not to mention our own doughnuts," Jan grinned, lifting the lid of the small toaster oven to let the sweet fragrance of doughnuts escape. "Have one."

"Jan, you angel! I came without breakfast this morning, and all I got for lunch was half a club sandwich, and no dessert . . ."

Jan watched her munch happily on the doughnut. "Which you didn't have time for, I gather. Doesn't he feed you?"

She laughed. "I was too busy talking to eat, that's all."

"Miss Summer!"

Abby jumped. That deep roar was as familiar as

her face in the mirror. She put down the coffee cup and ran for the door. It must be something terrible to make him bellow like that on a full stomach.

She opened the door to McCallum's office without stopping long enough to knock. "Yes, sir?" she asked breathlessly, her face flushed, her hair disheveled.

He glared at her, and his silver eyes had the cold brilliance of ice in the sun. "What the hell is this?" he demanded, glancing down at the pad in his big hand. " 'His cruel mouth fastened on her soft . . .' "

"No!" she screamed, making a dive for the legal pad. She jerked it out of his light grasp and clutched it possessively to her breast, staring horrified at him over the top of it. "It's mine!"

"Then where is mine?" he asked sharply. "All my notes on that burglary involved in the White murder case were on it, and it's gone!"

"But it was on your desk Friday when I locked up," she protested. "Maybe Jerry picked it up by accident when he took that brief to court this morning."

He was still scowling at her. His big body was poised on the edge of the swivel chair that was just barely adequate for his massive size.

"Are you sure that isn't mine?" he persisted gruffly.

She thumbed through the pages, and found each one covered with her own high scrawl. "No, I'm positive, it's definitely not yours," she replied. The thought of his eyes on that torrid love scene made her want to go down under the carpet. Nothing could have been more embarrassing.

"Damn it, I need those notes." He drew in a deep, short breath. "Well, why isn't Jerry back? Where is he?"

"I don't know . . ."

"Don't just stand there, damn it, find him!" he grumbled. "Call the courthouse, talk to the clerk, see if he left word where he was going. Ask Jan, maybe she knows, but find him!"

She closed the door softly behind her and leaned against it to get her breath. It was like closing the door between herself and a hungry lion, and the relief was equally great. This fierce, angry man was reminiscent of the old McCallum she'd met head-on during her first week in the office. He'd mellowed just a little since then, but something had sprung the lock on his impatient temper, and she sincerely hoped that he wouldn't carry it home with him. If he did, it was going to be an impossible two weeks.

She went back to the conference room, where Jan was waiting, wide-eyed, and picked up her coffee and her doughnut. He could just wait while she finished her coffee, temper or no temper. Heaven knew, he worked her hard enough to deserve a break now and then.

"What's going on?" Jan asked, glancing at the

legal pad Abby had placed on the shiny conference table.

"McCallum got my legal pad by mistake," Abby grimaced, remembering. "Do you know where Jerry is? I've got to find him or I'm going to be cut to ribbons."

"He had to see a client this afternoon," Jan said, watching her friend gulp coffee and cram half a doughnut into her mouth. "He should be yelling at me, not you. You're going to live with him."

"Oh, I just can't wait!" Abby said in her best theatrical voice. "It will be like living among mistreated tigers."

Jan looked at her out of the corner of her eyes. "I'll draw you up a will, if you like."

"Do you know where Jerry's client lives?"

"At the county jail." Jan grinned. "You can call that dashing Lieutenant James, you know him. He'll find Jerry and have him phone in."

"Lieutenant James is sixty," Abby observed. "His dashing days are past." She gulped down her coffee. "However, a retired dasher is better than nothing. Thanks for the coffee."

"Next time, I'll dissolve some vitamin pills in it," Jan called after her.

Even with Lieutenant James's help, it took ten minutes for Abby to get in touch with Jerry. Her nerves weren't soothed by the fact that McCallum stood over her the whole time, wearing ruts in the carpet under his elegant shoes.

"You sound frantic, Abby," Jerry laughed when he answered. "What's wrong?"

"Have you got Mr. McCallum's legal pad?" she asked. Her voice sounded breathless, but she couldn't help it. McCallum was standing less than two feet away with blazing gray eyes.

"His legal pad? Just a minute, let me go and check my briefcase. Hold on . . ."

"He's checking," Abby told McCallum.

He didn't even speak. His face was like steel, and about as readable. His eyes slid idly down her body, and back up again. She tried not to notice, but her pulse went wild at the scrutiny.

"Yes, Abby, I've got it," Jerry said a minute later. "Does he need it right away? I'll be through here in about ten minutes and I can come straight back."

She looked up at McCallum. "He's got it. Can you wait ten minute while he finishes with his client?"

He rammed his big hands into his pockets. "He can have twenty—to get here."

"Mr. McCallum will expect you in his office in twenty minutes, Jerry," she said sweetly.

"Giving you hell, is he?" came the knowing reply. "I'll be there. Bye."

She put down the receiver. "Is there anything else, sir?" she asked with her professional voice.

"Only one," he replied, shouldering away from the door facing. "When a man's mouth fastens on that portion of a woman's anatomy, it's better for both of them if it isn't 'cruel,' " he murmured, tossing her a glance that contained equal parts of impatience and humor.

He went into his office and closed the door.

Abby quickly slid the legal pad into her desk drawer and started working on the letters McCallum had dictated after lunch.

CHAPTER THREE

It was almost quitting time when she remembered that she hadn't called Nick, McCallum's first order of the day. She was wary of antagonizing him any further, so she jerked up the phone and dialed his mother's number.

Four rings later, a sleepy voice mumbled, "Hello?"

Relief flooded through Abby's body. At least he hadn't caught the plane yet. "Nicky?"

"Abby?" He seemed to wake up all at once. "What's wrong?"

"Oh, nothing, just an order from the top," she murmured dryly. "The boss says to cancel your flight to Paris or else. He didn't mention what the 'or else' might be."

"He doesn't have to, I already know," Nicky sighed. "He won't have to start wielding his sword, I've already canceled it."

"Oh, Nicky, why do you let him tell you what to do?" she groaned.

She could hear the grin in his voice. "Because, my friend, Collette is still in town. She doesn't go home until next week. *Then* I'll follow her home."

"Good boy!" she laughed.

"When are you going to come see us?" he asked. "I'll take you riding. I'll even let you ride Grey's horse, if you promise not to tell."

That brought to mind the lie that was very shortly going to make the rounds of the office. She hesitated, wondering how to break the news to Nicky, and how she was going to face Mandy McCallum after it was out in the open.

"What's gotten into you?" Nicky prodded. "You sound strange."

She chewed on her lower lip. "Nicky, what would you say if I told you I was moving in with your brother?"

"That you must be desperate for a roommate," he replied immediately. "Are you really? For the obvious reason?"

She swallowed. "Yes."

He hesitated. "Scared?" he teased.

"Terrified!"

He laughed delightedly. "I wondered if he was going to stay blind forever. Now that it's come to a head, remind me to tell you what he said to me after our Christmas party," he added mysteriously. "Don't be nervous, Abby, he doesn't yell nearly as much at home as he does at work. Mother will be beside herself," he added, as if the thought tickled him madly.

"She won't be shocked . . . ?"

"At Grey?!" he burst out. "She'll be convinced that he's finally ready to settle down. You know how possessive Grey is about his privacy. The mere fact that he's willing to let you share it says a lot."

She felt her spine tingle and looked around to find McCallum watching her. He moved so silently for such a big man. It was unnerving.

"Time to go home," he told her, eyeing the phone. "Who are you talking to?"

"Nicky," she said involuntarily.

He moved forward, holding out his hand for the receiver. She gave it to him without an argument. "Nick?" he asked curtly. "If you get on that plane . . . you aren't? Fine, we'll talk about it later. Tell Mother I'm bringing Abby down for supper tomorrow night. Did you? Yes, you're right, she is. See you." He hung up, leaving Abby to wonder what he was talking about.

"Well, are you coming or not?" he asked curtly. "It's been a damned long day and I'm tired."

Without another word, she got up and put on her light coat, covered the typewriter, and picked up her purse. She called good-bye to Jan and Jerry, and waved at George Doppler as they passed his office. When the door closed behind them, she heard scurrying footsteps, and she knew Jan was on her way to tell the others the news. She sighed. Well, at least everybody knew, now. That was the hump, and she was over it.

Mrs. McDougal had dinner on the table minutes after they walked into McCallum's apartment. She smiled and nodded at Abby, a strange, appraising look in her blue eyes as she moved around the table to place their meal on it.

"Everything's fixed, and your dessert is on the stove," she said after a minute. She went to get her coat, whipping it easily around her ample girth. "Now, just leave those dishes, Miss Abby, I'll get them in the morning." She nodded her silver head, winked at Abby, smiled mischievously at McCallum, and slid out the door like an oversize fairy.

They were alone. And Abby's uneasiness seemed to make McCallum's short temper even shorter.

"For God's sake, will you stop pacing and sit down?" he demanded curtly, taking his place at the head of the table with unconscious grace.

"Yes, sir," she said, deciding that it might be best to humor him.

"Don't call me sir."

"No, sir."

"Abby!"

She reached for her coffee cup, lifting it in unsteady hands. It had already been a traumatic day, but this was getting rough. She took a deep breath and sipped her hot black coffee.

"She knows?" she asked softly.

"McDougal?" he grumbled. "Yes, she knows. My God, couldn't you tell? All those twinkling glances and sickening winks and smiles . . . she's positive that I'm head over heels in love."

"Poor, demented soul," she said in her most serious tone, meeting his eyes levelly.

He glared at her over a mound of mashed potatoes. "Pass the potatoes," he growled.

"You're already dishing them up," she pointed out.

"Then pass me the rolls!"

She did, smothering the uproarious laughter that was clamoring for escape. She ate the rest of the meal in silence, her mind quickly losing its sense of humor at the taciturn, smoldering look on his broad face. It wasn't going to work, that was already evident. He hated having her around. She was going to cost him his privacy, his love life, and subject him to the kind of teasing that would assault his dignity. She'd never dreamed the subterfuge would have such sweeping repercussions. She wondered if he hadn't considered the consequences when he made his gallant offer. It wasn't like McCallum to do anything on impulse, without thinking the action through. It was that attention to detail that made him such a fine attorney.

"We can still call it off," she said after she'd served

up the delicious cherry flan Mrs. McDougal had provided for dessert.

He put down his fork with cold deliberation, and she knew with a shiver that she'd finally given him the opening he was waiting for. His eyes glittered like shards of metal.

"Isn't it a little late for that?" he asked curtly. "The word's out, in case you've forgotten. Vinnie wailing all over me on the phone, Nick making cute remarks, Mrs. McDougal sighing like cupid on Valentine's Day . . . My God, if I'd had any idea what I was letting myself in for. . . ."

"I'll go right now," Abby said soothingly. "I'll call Miss Nichols and Nick myself. Everything will work out fine." She put down her napkin and left the table. It was almost a relief. The way he was acting, even having to face Robert Dalton wouldn't be a fraction of the strain.

She'd just opened the top drawer of her bureau to start taking out neatly folded tops and blouses when he paused in the doorway.

"Abby . . ." he began hesitantly.

"It's all right, really," she assured him. "It's probably for the best. I can get a job with the wire services and ask for an assignment to Central America . . ."

"You're breaking my heart," he growled.

She glared at him. "A lot you'd care if I got shot down in the streets," she muttered.

"It would depend on how much of my correspondence you'd answered," he replied matter-of-factly.

She wanted to throw something at him. The only problem was that she wasn't quite sure how he'd retaliate.

"Calm down, Abby," he chuckled.

She tossed back her long hair impatiently. "Calm down! How can I? You make me feel as welcome as a typhoid carrier. I realize that I'm in your way, and I'm sorry, but this was your idea, not mine."

"I know." He moved into the room, taking the blouse out of her hands. He tossed it lightly on top of the chest of drawers and caught her by the shoulders to study her.

"I've lived alone most of my life since I came out of the service," he said quietly. "Adjusting to another person is never easy. You might remember that from your marriage."

"I didn't have to adjust to Gene," she said bitterly. "He was never at home."

He paused. "Other women?"

"Yes. Other women."

His fingers tightened before he let her go and moved away. "Come and drink some coffee with me. Then you'll have to amuse yourself. I've got some phone calls to make."

"I don't expect to be entertained," she murmured as they walked back to the living room. "I'm used to being alone, too. I have a manuscript I work on in the evenings."

"The one about the man with the cruel mouth and the 'wise, patient hands'?" he asked, tongue in cheek.

She hated the ruby blush that highlighted her high cheekbones. "Fie on you, counselor," she grumbled. "One of these days, I'm going to sell that book, and you'll be laughing through your teeth."

He chuckled deeply. "I hope you can write to music. I rarely watch anything on television except the evening news."

"Neither do I," she admitted. She glanced at him nervously. "There's one show on this week that I've just got to watch, though," she said hesitantly. "I'll turn it down very low . . ."

He looked irritated. "Well, which one? A soap opera, no doubt."

She glared at him. "No, it isn't. It's a special on public television about a dig in Egypt . . ."

"In the Valley of the Kings?" he asked sharply. "The one about the site that had to be moved because of the Aswan Dam?"

She felt shocked. "Why, yes."

"I've seen it once, but I'll gladly sit through it again with you." He moved to the record player, his eyes puzzled. "Is that a fluke, or do you like archaeology?"

"I'm nuts about it," she admitted. "I read every book I can find on the subject. I subscribe to magazines about it, I watch all the specials."

"So do I," he admitted with a slow smile. "When you're not writing the Great American Novel, dig into my bookshelves," he nodded toward the bookcase that lined the walls. "I've got some excellent volumes with pages of color photos, all on Egypt, Greece, Mexico, Peru . . ."

"I'll never get any writing done," she wailed, her eyes greedy on the titles as she walked down the row of subjects. "Oh, how wonderful . . . !"

"Do you like Rachmaninoff?" he murmured as he started the cassette player and the rich strains filled the room.

"The Second Piano Concerto? I love it," she murmured, her already buried in a thick text on the Inca civilization.

He laughed softly as he went toward his study in what would have been a third bedroom before its bed was replaced by a desk. "I think we'll get along all right," he murmured.

The next evening they had supper with McCallum's mother and brother, and if she'd expected them to be shocked, she was in for a surprise.

"I've seen it coming for months," Mandy said with a quiet smile, her dark hair and gray eyes leaving no doubt about which of his parents McCallum favored the most. She was a tall woman, but slender, and the blue dress she was wearing flattered her. "I wasn't even surprised when Nicky told me."

"Neither was I," Nicky grinned, glancing from McCallum's taciturn face to Abby's smiling one. Nicky was as different from his brother as midnight from dawn. He had light brown hair and blue eyes, and he was half Greyson McCallum's size.

"A likely story," Mandy teased. "Who was it who went around the house for ten minutes laughing about the irony of it? Didn't you also mention something about beauty and the . . ."

"How about some more coffee?" Nicky asked quickly. He jumped to his feet. "I'll get the pot."

"Anyway," Mandy continued, "Greyson, I do hope that this arrangement is only temporary. Marriage may be old-fashioned, but you just can't bring children into the world . . ."

"Children!" McCallum burst out.

Mandy glanced at him warily. "I did remember to tell you what caused them?"

It was the first time Abby could ever remember seeing him flustered. He was holding his coffee cup as if he expected it to try to escape. His face was stiff with indignation.

"Abby will want children, won't you, dear?" Mandy asked her gently.

Abby felt the question to her toes. Yes, she wanted them, she always had. But she'd never thought about them in connection with Greyson McCallum. Now she did. And it shocked her to discover that she wouldn't mind having his child. She stared at him with the shock of discovery in her eyes.

"Don't you recognize stark terror when you see it, Mother?" McCallum asked wryly, indicating Abby's face. "Not everyone thinks children are the ultimate pleasure in a relationship."

Mandy glanced up as Nicky came into the room with the percolator in his hand. "What took you so long?" she teased. "Was there a woman hiding in the closet?"

Abby burst out laughing. It would have been so in character for Nicky to have a girl friend hiding there, she couldn't help her reaction.

"You see?" Mandy laughed. "Abby wouldn't be surprised, either. Honestly, Nicky, why don't you think about starting a family as well? At this rate, I may not be around to spoil my first grandchild."

"Oh, I very much doubt that," McCallum said dryly.

Mandy made a face at him. "Have some more pudding, Abby. Pass it here, Nicky."

"You sweet little tyrant, you," Nicky teased as he handed over the dish.

The older woman smiled complacently. "I had to be to raise Greyson," she reminded him.

"Was he really that bad?" Abby had to ask.

Mandy studied her eldest with pure love in her eyes. "He was my anchor, my dear," she said in a sincere tone. "I don't think the family would have survived without him. We certainly wouldn't have had so much," she added, referring to the spacious home and its multiacred surroundings on the outskirts of the city.

"You'd have managed," Grey chuckled.

Nicky checked his watch. "Oops," he muttered, rising. "I've got to get going. I'm taking my best girl to the ballet."

"Best girl?" McCallum murmured suspiciously.

"Yes," Nicky said over his shoulder. "Collette's still in town, didn't Abby mention it?"

McCallum glared across the table at Abby. He didn't say a word, but she knew when they got back to the apartment that she was going to be on the receiving end of some unpleasant words.

And she was. They were no sooner inside the door when McCallum let loose with both barrels.

"Was there some special reason for not telling me about that French disaster?" he demanded.

She drew herself up and glared back at him. "Why should I? It's Nicky's business."

"Nicky's a boy."

"He's twenty-five and part owner of a public relations firm. When are you going to realize that he's a grown man?"

"When he begins to act like one," he shot back. "I've worked like hell to support my family, to keep it together. I'm not going to have it all go down the tube because Nicky's infatuated with some call girl!"

"She isn't a call girl!"

"How would you know?" he asked gruffly. His big hand shot out to jerk her roughly against his massive body. "You cold little piece of porcelain," he accused, "what would you know about women who exchange their bodies for favors?"

She stared up at him helplessly, her temper gone, her senses staggered by his sudden nearness.

He tangled one hand in her hair and pulled her head back slowly. "No wonder your husband went astray, Abby," he ground out as he bent his head. "You don't give an inch!"

His mouth crushed down on hers and hurt, the anger in it merciless as he twisted her soft lips under his to force them to part. His tongue shot into the sweet darkness of her mouth while his hands slid down her back to grip the backs of her thighs and grind her hips against his.

She gasped under his hard mouth at the intimate contact that she hadn't known in such a long time. She could feel every hard muscle of his thighs and stomach in that forced embrace as his hands relentlessly lifted her even closer into it. His mouth demanded, possessed, while she drew up inside at the unbridled fury she could taste in the overpowering ardor. He was hell-bent on his own pleasure, not knowing or caring if she was receiving anything from it.

"No," she begged against his hard mouth. "Grey, no, not in anger. Please . . ."

The pleading of her shaky voice seemed to bring him to his senses. He drew back, his eyes on her mouth while he slowed his breath. His big hands relaxed their rough hold on her thighs, sliding sensuously up over her hips to catch her by the waist.

She looked back at him with all the old feelings of inadequacy gripping her. His careless words had hurt. She'd always felt guilty that Gene had gone from her bed to other women's, but she hadn't been able to give him anything in a physical sense. She'd expected that side of marriage to fall automatically into place with the ring on her finger, but it hadn't. She'd only been infatuated, and Gene's rough treatment of her on their wedding night had been the first in a series of embarrassingly brief and unsatisfying encounters. Even though she'd tried naively to please her new husband, she'd never been able to give him passion. He'd accused her of being cold, and she'd accepted the criticism without protest, believing it to be true. When he'd asked for a divorce, she'd given it willingly. But the scars had remained with her, and now McCallum had reopened and rubbed salt in them.

"Let me go, please," she said in a choked voice.

He removed his hands absently, as if he hadn't even realized that they were still holding her.

She drew back from him, her eyes mirroring all the pain and fear that lingered.

"You were right, Mr. McCallum," she said in a tiny voice. "Your private life is none of my business. I . . . I won't forget again." She turned and walked briskly to the room he'd given her. Once inside, she locked the door behind her and the scalding tears ran freely down her cheeks.

She didn't sleep. Memories came back to taunt her, of Gene's late nights, his endless criticism of her as a woman. Why had McCallum chosen that particular way of getting even? He had the killer instinct to a frightening degree. It was what made him such a good criminal lawyer, because he wasn't afraid to hit where it hurt the most.

She dragged out of bed at five thirty, took her shower and dressed in a white pleated skirt and silky blouse, complemented by a navy blazer and matching navy pumps. She brushed her hair and put on the maximum of eye makeup. But the hollows under her eyes stood out despite her best efforts. She gathered her purse and went down the hall to the dining room.

McCallum, faultless in a pale brown business suit, was sitting quietly at the table while Mrs. McDougal spooned a panful of scrambled eggs into the serving dish and placed it on the table. There was already a plate of fresh biscuits and a platter of bacon on the polished surface of the hardwood table.

"Good morning," Abby told Mrs. McDougal with a wan smile.

"Good morning, love. Sit down and have breakfast. I'll pour the coffee as soon as I've put this pan in to soak." She vanished through the swinging door that led into the kitchen.

McCallum was buttering a biscuit, but his gray

eyes didn't miss much as they scanned Abby's face. "That was a nasty remark I made to you last night," he said quietly. "I apologize for it."

She forked a piece of bacon onto her own plate. "I had no right to comment on your personal affairs," she said quietly.

"That doesn't excuse me."

Her shoulders lifted and fell. "It doesn't matter. By the way, Jerry wants to know if I can go to the clerk's office with him this morning. He's got to get some information on a land transfer and he needs me to take it down as he dictates it."

There was a long pause. "All right. For an hour or two, no more. Dalton's coming this afternoon."

She felt her body stiffen. In all the emotional turmoil of the night before, she'd forgotten. Incredibly, she'd forgotten. "Yes," she murmured.

They ate breakfast in a tense silence, broken only by Mrs. McDougal's soft humming in the kitchen while she cleaned up the pots and pans. They had a last cup of coffee before they left for work. When they rose, and McCallum started to take her arm, she flinched.

His expression was indescribable. He held her all the same, staring down at her with a face that rivaled a diamond for hardness.

"That won't do, Abby," he said tautly. "We're not going to fool Dalton if you flinch every time I come near you."

"Sorry," she said, with an attempt at lightness. "I'll work on it night and day."

"I hurt you last night, didn't I?" he asked in a strange, deep tone.

She moved away from him to go in the living room and get her purse. "We'll be late," she said, but she wouldn't look at him.

He hesitated for an instant before he went to open the door for her.

She stayed out of his way until lunch, and then there was no avoiding him. He came out of his office with a determined look on his face and stood over her until she gave up on the letter she was trying to type and looked at him.

"It's noon. Let's get some lunch," he told her.

She fished for an excuse. "Uh, Jan was going with me . . ."

"I'm going with you," he corrected. "Now."

She knew the tone. It meant he was going to get his way if he had to pick her up and carry her out of the building. With a resigned sigh, she got her purse out of the drawer and went peaceably.

There was a small Italian restaurant a block from the office, tucked between a furniture store and a smart little boutique. In the middle of busy Atlanta, it was like finding a misplaced piece of Italy. There were red checkered tablecloths with candles in wine bottles and flowers on the tables, and a smiling proprietor who greeted guests while friendly waiters took orders.

The spaghetti was just right, and the garlic bread was a temptation Abby couldn't resist. She hadn't wanted to come with McCallum, but she was enjoying it despite her intentions.

"At least you don't starve yourself," he murmured as he sipped a second cup of coffee over an empty plate.

She glanced at him before she finished the last of her spaghetti. "I don't have to. I never gain."

"A few pounds wouldn't hurt you," he replied. His eyes studied what was visible of her slender body above the table, narrow and appraising.

She ignored the look. "Thank you for lunch," she said, and leaned back with her coffee cupped in her hands. "It was delicious."

"I'm glad you enjoyed it." He lit a cigarette and studied her through the smoke. "I want to explain something to you. I want you to understand why I'm so concerned about Nicky."

She flushed uncomfortably. "You don't owe me any explanations, Mr. McCallum," she said tautly.

"My father committed suicide when I was sixteen."

She tried to speak and couldn't. Her eyes looked into his helplessly.

"My father was a sharecropper," he said quietly, "a farmer who gets a share of the profits he makes on rented land. He'd saved all his life to buy a tract of land all his own and get out of debt. He'd just managed that when Mother got pregnant with Nicky. There were complications, and he only had life insurance, no health insurance. He had to sell the land to meet the debts, but that was only the beginning. By the time Nicky was born, the bills amounted to more than Dad could make sharecropping in twenty years, even if he'd been blessed with perfect weather." He took a long draw from the cigarette. "He took a stab at it, he tried. But eventually the hopelessness of the situation depressed him to the extent that he began to drink. Nicky was a year old the night Dad took his old army revolver out onto the front porch and blew his brains out."

She'd wondered many times why McCallum was as strong as he was—and now that iron in his make-up began to make sense.

"How did you manage?" she asked.

His face grew hard. "On the charity of one of Mother's uncles. For the last year I was in school. After that, I went into the army and had an allotment made out for Mother and Nicky. I stayed in four years during Vietnam, got a job on a construction gang when I got my discharge and went through law school at night. A few years later I began to make a living," he chuckled, and Abby knew what he meant. It was hard finding a good law firm to join with a law degree that didn't come from full-time status as a student. Although McCallum had managed it very well. "A stint in the D. A.'s office as a prosecuting attorney got me where I am," he added. "But what it adds up to is this. I backed Nicky in that public relations firm he owns half of. He's getting his head above water for the first time and I want him to keep it there. A woman, especially one who likes expensive trinkets, could bankrupt him overnight. Now do you understand? Mother will always be my responsibility, and I don't mind it a bit. But Nicky needs to stand on his own. It's past time."

She felt vaguely ashamed of herself. "I see," she said quietly. "And I'm sorry I spoke out of turn. I thought you came from a moneyed background, I didn't realize . . ." She shifted restlessly.

"Silver spoons and a white-coated butler?" he mused. "I could afford them, now. But I don't have the inclination for status symbols, or much patience with people who deal in them."

"I wish you wouldn't judge people so harshly on first impressions, that's all," she continued softly. "Collette is such a sweet girl. . . ." She glanced at him and away. "I . . . I may be porcelain," she said with a bitter laugh, "but I'm not all that bad at summing up people. Reporters learn that trick along with lead sentences. She struck me as a very sheltered young lady on her own for the first time."

He studied her averted face for a long time. "Are you ever going to forgive me for calling you that?" he asked in a deep, gentle tone.

"Why should I have to?" Her laugh was bitter. "It was true."

He caught her hand in his and ignored her feeble attempt to drag it away. "You've never talked about your marriage," he said, watching her. "It left scars, didn't it? Did he accuse you of being cold, Abby? Is that the excuse he used to have other women?"

"No fair, counselor," she said coldly, jerking her hand away. Her lower lip thrust forward accusingly. "That's badgering." She stood up. "Please, can we go?"

He stood up with a hard sigh, crushing his cigarette in the ashtray. "What's the matter, honey, did I hit too close to the truth?" he asked with a hard laugh as he went to pay the check.

She didn't even answer him. Her voice would have wobbled if she'd tried, with mingled anger and indignation. McCallum, she decided, would try the patience of a saint.

She found excuses to help Jerry or Jan for the rest of the day. Anything to keep out of McCallum's way. It was puzzling that she'd managed to get along with him so well until these past two days. It was like being in a combat zone, now that she was living with him. She was grateful that Dalton was coming. It would be like having the cavalry come over the hill! At least Robert had never thought she was cold. . . .

It was almost four o'clock on the nose when he

walked into the waiting room and came face-to-face with Abby.

He seemed to contract all over, standing statue-still in the doorway, his pale eyes wide with shock.

"Abby!" he exclaimed.

CHAPTER FOUR

He hadn't changed a lot in one year. He was much the same as she remembered him, tall and very dignified. Utterly charming. But her reaction to him was different. It confused her. She'd expected to be wildly flustered and attracted. And she wasn't.

"Abby," he repeated softly, shock in the handsome face she remembered so well. "My God, what are you doing here?"

"Working," she said dryly. She got up and extended her hand. Amazing how easy it was to be friendly and nothing more. "It's nice to see you again, Mr. Dalton."

"Robert," he corrected. He clasped her hand between both of his. His eyes made a meal of her face. "Abby, I've wondered all this time where you went, how you were. I felt like ten kinds of a heel after what I put you through . . . Abby, you'll never know how I hated myself for that cowardly display."

He'd never know how she'd hated him, or how she'd wanted revenge for it. He'd never know how he'd hurt her. But somewhere in the months since it had happened, she'd become wrapped up in McCallum's world. Charleston had retreated into the past, like a dimly remembered nightmare.

"It was a long time ago, Robert," she said gently. Her green eyes studied him. She'd forgotten that he was almost twenty years her senior. His blond hair had a liberal sprinkling of silver and there were deep lines beside his eyes and mouth. But the charm was still there, and the tenderness. He wasn't sensual like McCallum, but he had appeal.

"Yes, a long time ago," he agreed. His pale blue eyes searched her face. "Liz and I are separated now," he said slowly. "You brought all the problems to a head. We worked out a settlement just two weeks later." He sighed heavily. "I tried to find you, but you'd vanished. Abby, perhaps now . . ."

Before he could suggest what he was thinking, McCallum's office door opened and he came through it, his narrow silver eyes darting from Abby to Dalton.

"Hello, Robert," he said formally, extending his hand. "Good to see you."

"Same here, Grey," he replied cordially, glancing warmly at Abby. "I've just been renewing my acquaintance with your charming secretary. We knew each other in Charleston."

"Did you?" McCallum asked.

Dalton's eyes caught Abby's. "I was just telling her about my separation from Liz. I thought I might be able to persuade her to join me for dinner this evening."

The expression that darkened McCallum's face was an open threat. He moved closer to Abby almost imperceptibly, one big arm sliding around her shoulders in a gesture that was possessive as well as supportive.

"I don't think so," he said. His voice was deep and measured—his courtroom voice.

Dalton seemed to shrink. "Oh?"

McCallum's glittering silver eyes dropped to Abby's face with something resembling hunger. "However, we'd both enjoy having you join us for dinner this evening at our apartment," he said frankly. "Wouldn't we, Abby?"

"Of course," she agreed, mainly because she couldn't bear the thought of another evening alone with McCallum. Since their confrontation the night before, she was wary of him.

She felt the arm around her contract as if in bridled anger, but she didn't try to pull away.

"I'd like that," Dalton said. "What time?"

"About seven." McCallum gave Abby a long look and turned toward his office. "Come on in. I'll give you directions to the apartment before we discuss this deal." He closed the door behind them, and Dalton still hadn't regained his composure. It gave Abby a tiny nudge of pleasure. She went back to her desk smiling.

The silence in McCallum's apartment would have been deafening without Mrs. McDougal's pleasant chatter while she prepared a delicious steak dinner, complete with homemade rolls and a superb spinach salad, and apple pie and cream for dessert.

McCallum's narrow eyes were tracing Abby like an artist's brush on a canvas. She was wearing a slinky taffeta dress, long skirted with a nipped waist, black spaghetti straps and a fitted, low-cut bodice with corselet ties that left a strip of skin acutely bare down to her waist. She'd worn it in defiance, to show him that she did know how to dress to catch a man's eye. But she hadn't counted on catching his to this extent. Her fingers went nervously to her high-piled coiffure, to the dangling gold shimmer of her earrings.

He himself was striking in dark evening clothes. It was the first time they'd dressed for dinner, and it would serve Dalton right if he showed up in a sports coat, she thought amusedly.

"Martini, Abby?" he asked after a minute, rising from his seat on the sofa to go to the bar.

She shook her head. "But I'd love a glass of wine if you have it." She sat down in the chair beside the sofa, careful not to wrinkle the elegant skirt of her dress.

"Sweet, no doubt," he teased lightly, glancing at her. "The only thing I have is a very dry sherry. How about brandy?"

"That would be nice, thank you."

"Nervous?" he asked. He poured the amber liquid into a snifter and turned to pour himself a whiskey before he brought it to her.

"Just a little," she admitted with a shy smile. But because of you, not of Robert, she added to herself.

He sat down across from her, crossing one long, powerful leg over the other. "Afraid to sit by me?" he taunted.

"I . . . I'm just being careful of my dress," she lied, straightening the skirt. "Taffeta wrinkles easily."

He sipped the whiskey. "Was it as bad as you expected, seeing him again?"

She shook her head. "Not nearly." She sipped the brandy slowly. "He hasn't changed."

"He's a great deal older than you," he observed.

"Twenty years."

He leaned back on the sofa, his head slightly to one side as he studied her. "Was his age the main attraction?" he asked gruffly.

Her eyes jerked up. "I beg your pardon?"

"Did you think he wouldn't be too demanding in bed?"

She felt the blood rush to her face as the question penetrated to her mind. Slamming the snifter down on the table as she got to her feet. "You abominable . . . !"

"What's the matter, honey, did I hit a nerve?" he broke in, rising to tower over her, his eyes narrow and calculating. "Come on, Abby, talk. Were you looking for a man who wouldn't pose a threat to you sexually? Are you afraid of sex?"

She started blindly past him, with some wild idea of staying in her room until Dalton got there. Thank goodness Mrs. McDougal was out of earshot . . .

But McCallum, for so large a man, was incredibly light on his feet. Before she could get away, he was in front of her, barring the way.

"No, you don't," he said calmly. "No more running. I want to know, and you're going to tell me."

"Oh, no, I'm not," she shot back at him, her stance pure bravado. "I don't owe you that kind of answer, counselor."

"But I'm going to get it," he said in his courtroom voice. He moved forward like an uncoiling spring to catch her by the waist, holding her helplessly before him. "What was the attraction, Abby?" he kept on relentlessly. His glittering eyes filled the room, filled the world, his fingers around her waist hurt. "A man old enough to be your father . . ."

"You almost are!" she hit back, wanting to wound in return.

"Nice try, honey," he laughed shortly, "but not good enough. Are you frigid, Abby?"

"All right!" she cried, shaking with mingled fury and pain. Tears rushed into her dark green eyes. "All right, yes, I'm frigid, is that what you want? I cringed every time my husband touched me, until one day he left and didn't come back!"

His eyes studied her pale, tear-washed face quietly. The fingers on her waist became tender, caressing. "Didn't you want him?" he asked quietly.

Her eyes closed, squeezing out the rest of the gathered tears. She sniffed and took a steadying breath. Just to talk about it was a relief beyond words, she'd held it in for so long.

"No," she whispered, admitting it at last. "No, I didn't want him in any physical way. I thought I loved him." She laughed. "I thought he loved me. I didn't realize that all he wanted was a more important position with my father's bank. He thought marrying me would accomplish it."

"Did it?"

She shook her head. "Bank presidents don't get that far up the ladder without being able to size up employees. Gene didn't have managerial ability, and Dad knew it. He never really cared for Gene. Mother didn't, either. They tolerated him, for my sake."

"You never talk about your parents, either."

She smiled wetly, taking the handkerchief he offered and wiping her face with it. "They live in Panama City, and I dote on them. I miss them too much to talk about them. I get homesick."

He laughed softly. "I'll fly you down one day soon."

She crumpled the handkerchief in a small fist against his evening jacket, staring up at him curiously. "I don't understand you."

"Why? Because I force things out of you that you don't want to admit—not even to yourself?" He drew her closer, until her thighs felt the hard warmth of his, even through the layers of fabric. "I'm insatiably curious, Abby," he murmured. "Digging out secrets is my profession."

"I have a right to privacy," she reminded him.

"Not with me you don't," he told her, something dark and soft in his tone. He had an actor's voice, he could shade it in a dozen different ways to reflect anger, command, indignation. But this shade was like velvet, rich and smooth, and it affected her in strange ways.

"You . . . there are things you don't need to know," she protested. The warmth of his big body, the elusive fragrance of his cologne, were making deep impressions, weakening her.

"I need to know everything," he replied. One big hand moved up between them, a darkly beautiful hand with flat, immaculate nails and a sprinkling of hairs on its back. It toyed with the string of the first bow that held her bodice together and slowly, lazily, tugged until it came loose.

Abby's breath caught at the back of her throat. She looked up at him in disbelief, not moving, not speaking. Her eyes looked into his, searchingly, as he repeated the action with the second bow. There was only one left, but already she felt the coolness of the room against her bare skin.

"The advantage of small breasts," he said very softly, easing a long finger into the opening to touch, lightly, the hard, pink peak of one breast, "is that you don't need to bother with a bra."

She felt the color burn into her face, and wondered at the effect he was having on her. Her slender body began to tremble delicately, and a tiny part of her mind wondered why she was permitting this kind of intimacy.

The other hand speared into the hair at the nape of her neck, where it was swept up into the sophisticated topknot. He unfastened it with deliberate movements, watching it tumble down around her shoulders.

"Don't put it up again," he said. "I like it like this, long and sexy." His eyes dropped to her bodice, where that maddening finger was tracing a fiery path against her breast.

"Grey . . ." she whispered, her lips parting, her eyes half closed as the touch aroused sensations long forgotten.

His mouth brushed against hers softly, teasingly. His finger touched and lifted inside the bodice, and she realized belatedly that her body was twisting, lifting toward it, trying to capture it against the swelling softness of her breast.

One big hand ran down her spine to her buttocks, pressing her lips into intimate contact with the hardening muscles of his own. "What do you want, Abby?" he whispered against her trembling mouth.

"Want . . . ?" she echoed in an unsteady whisper.

He chuckled softly, dangerously against her parting lips, his mouth easing sensuously between them as his warm fingers suddenly burrowed lazily under the bodice to take the weight of her breast, his palm pressing deeply against the taut, aching nipple.

A strange, high-pitched whimper broke out of her throat and whispered into his mouth.

He drew back a breath to look down at her, his silver eyes taking in the wildness of her dilating green eyes, the drawn look in her cheeks. "Now, that's sexy," he murmured. He bent to brush his mouth over hers tantalizingly.

"What . . . is?" she managed, not even bothering to protest the possessive hand cupping her breast.

"That wild little sound you just made," he replied, "not to mention the way your body is melting against mine."

She hadn't realized that it was, but all at once she felt the hardness of his thighs where hers were lifting and falling, and she tensed.

"Self-conscious?" He lifted his head and looked down at the bodice of her gown, where the black fabric showed up the skin of his wrist. His fingers moved, sliding half of the bodice completely away from her high, firm breast to bare it to his narrowed eyes. "My God, your skin is fair," he murmured, noticing the contrast of his dark fingers against the whiteness of her soft flesh.

Her cheek was resting on his shoulder, her eyes watching him helplessly while her heart threatened to beat itself to death. It had never been like this before, she'd never been vulnerable like this with any man.

"No protests?" he whispered gently. His eyes searched hers while his fingers stroked her, feeling the trembling softness lift toward them. "Suppose I do this, Abby . . ." With a smooth, deft movement, he drew the other strap down her arm until the bodice fell to her waist. Both big, warm hands swallowed her then, his thumbs flicking the taut nipples, his eyes strangely watchful on her face.

"Oh, Grey," she whispered, her aching voice a stranger's, her hands trembling as she reached up to lock them behind his broad neck and pressed herself against him. "Don't—don't stop."

"Like this?" His big hands contracted gently, caressing, probing. His mouth opened over hers, nudging it softly, his tongue teasing, tracing the long line of her lips before it shot into her mouth, no longer teasing. "Unbutton my shirt," he ground out. "I want to feel your bare skin against mine."

"Mrs. . . . McDougal . . ." she whispered brokenly.

He muttered something, lifting his head. His breath was coming as erratically as hers, she could feel the roughness of his heartbeat against her.

Without a word, he caught her by the hand and pulled her into the room he used for a study, closing the door firmly behind him. His eyes lanced over her bare breasts while his fingers tore at the tie, tossing it into a chair before they flicked open the buttons over his hair-roughened chest.

"Now," he muttered, lifting her body against his, watching her taut nipples vanish in the thick nest of hair over his muscular chest. "Oh, God, now . . . !" His head bent to her smooth shoulders, his mouth insistent as it slid roughly against the silky skin, burning where it touched.

Abby could barely breathe at all. Her arms were locked around him, her head thrown back, her eyes closed as she let her body drown in sensation. The pleasure was so intense it made her ache. She moved restlessly, dragging her breasts against his hard chest, the thick hair tickling, deliciously abrasive against the tender flesh.

"Cold?" he ground out, his voice husky, faintly unsteady. "My God . . . !" His mouth slid down to cover one taut nipple, his tongue hard against it, his lips swallowing it, savoring it.

She held his head against her rigid body, her fingers digging into the nape of his strong neck. "Grey," she whispered achingly, "Grey, I ache so . . . !"

His mouth slid up her body, all the way up to cover her lips. His hands slid down, lifting her by the thighs until her hips were crushed against his blatant masculinity, letting her feel the arousal she could taste on his demanding mouth.

She trembled wildly against him. Her fingers tangled in the thick hair on his chest, tugging at it sensuously while his mouth drained hers in a silence that pulsed with hunger. Her breath rasped, mingling with the unnatural tenor of his.

"Do you know how much I want you, Abby?" he asked in a deep, harsh tone.

"I . . . thought you didn't want me," she whispered against his mouth, " . . . before."

His fingers bit into her soft thighs, pressing her sensuously to him. "You can feel how much I want you now," he murmured huskily. "I want you naked in my arms, Abby," he whispered achingly. "I want to warm every inch of you, I want to hear you crying out with the pleasure I'm going to give you . . ."

Her eyes looked straight into his, misty with the hungers he'd aroused. "Take me to bed, Grey," she whispered softly. "Make love to me."

His big body shuddered with the words, his eyes blazing into hers, his hands contracting, hurting her. "Now?" he whispered roughly.

"Now," she whispered back. She leaned forward and traced his firm, chiseled mouth with just the tip of her tongue.

The sudden blast of the doorbell's loud chime was like a spray of ice water. Abby jerked in his embrace, stunned at the interruption.

McCallum bit off a harsh curse. He let Abby slide

down his body until her feet touched the floor, but he still held her to him. His arms drew her close, comforting now, soothing. His hands on her bare back were faintly trembling.

"Dalton, no doubt," he murmured in her hair.

She stiffened. "Mrs. McDougal won't . . . come in here, will she?" she asked nervously.

He chuckled softly and caught her shoulders, moving her away from him just enough to give his glittering eyes access to her high, swollen breasts.

"Poor Dalton," he murmured, staring boldly at the soft curves.

Passion had sliced away her inhibitions, but with the return of sanity came self-consciousness. She drew back, her nervous fingers drawing the bodice back in place.

He laughed softly, watching her fumble with the ties while he fastened his shirt and replaced his tie.

"Embarrassed, Abby?" he chided.

She couldn't find the courage to meet his eyes. She was embarrassed, all right, but more than that she was shocked. That uninhibited woman Grey had released had been a complete stranger to her.

She tied the last bow and drew in a long, steadying breath.

"Oh, Mr. McCallum, your company's here!" Mrs. McDougal's voice burst down the long hall toward the bedrooms.

McCallum chuckled softly as Abby worked at her tangled hair with her fingers.

"Leave it, honey," he said softly, coming up behind her to catch her by the shoulders. "You look like you've been making love, which is exactly the impression I wanted Dalton to get."

Something went cold inside her. "Was . . . was that why?" she asked, steadying her voice.

"What do you think?" he asked carelessly.

She turned around, her green eyes dark and sensuous, her lips rosy from the long, sweet contact with his, her hair disheveled but flattering. "I think you're dangerous," she said.

One corner of his chiseled mouth went up; his amused eyes searched hers. "You might keep it in mind the next time you wear a dress like that," he told her, studying the bows with a devastating boldness. "Those damned bows are a temptation no man can resist."

The words brought back the feel of his slightly rough hands on her velvety skin, and her breathing accelerated just enough to be visible.

"I thought self-restraint was something you learned in law school," she muttered.

"It only applies to law, honey, not to women. Except in one respect," he added, with a slow, sensuous smile. "Would you like me to explain that?"

She could feel the heat in her cheeks. "No, thanks." She turned toward the door. "Robert will wonder where we are."

"Not when he gets a look at you, Miss Summer," he said with a soft laugh.

She glared at him over one bare shoulder. "I think you're despicable," she grumbled.

Both dark eyebrows lifted toward the ceiling. "Can this be the same passionate woman who, less than five minutes ago, was begging me to take her to bed?"

She could have strangled him. Words boiled up into her mouth, but couldn't manage to get out.

"Think of it this way," he murmured, as he moved to her side to open the door. "A good writer draws upon experience. And now you'll have something to draw upon, won't you?" And he opened the door and went through it before she could get past her involuntary gasp.

The look in Robert Dalton's eyes when he saw Abby was something she couldn't describe. The tall, dignified man seemed to age all at once when he saw the telltale marks of McCallum's violent lovemaking on her face.

"Abby, how lovely you look," he said with genuine appreciation, moving forward to take both her hands in his and study her, smiling. "You make me feel my age."

"Oh, I make Mr. McCallum feel his, too," Abby murmured with a glance in her boss's direction that earned her a black scowl.

"Mr. McCallum?" Dalton teased lightly.

"She's called me worse," McCallum muttered.

"Greyson," she warned, glaring at him.

He only grinned. "Would you like a martini, Bob, or something stronger?"

"A brandy would do me," the older man replied with a smile. He was still watching Abby with a steady, intense gaze. "I can't get over the change," he said quietly.

"I'm older," she agreed.

"That wasn't what I meant." His eyes grew sad. "How long have you and Grey been . . . together?"

"Over a year," McCallum said, pausing to retrieve Abby's snifter and hand it to her as he brought Dalton's drink.

"We, uh, we haven't been living together that long, though," Abby murmured, accepting the glass with a smile.

"Oh?" Dalton brightened.

McCallum's eyes narrowed. "We would have been, if I'd managed to turn the heat up far enough," he murmured quietly, staring at her.

"How is the shipping business?" Abby asked Dalton quickly.

"Oh, I've ditched my interests," he said pleasantly. "I sold out to Liz. Now I'm more interested in real estate. I own a chain of realty companies, and Grey, as I'm sure you know, has a well-run construction operation. We're trying to work out a deal, and let Grey's brother build us an image."

No, Abby hadn't known because McCallum was as tight-lipped as a clam about his private business.

Abby was privy only to what concerned the legal practice.

"Bob's secretary has been handling the paperwork," McCallum said. He moved to Abby's side and drew her up against him with a casual motion that wasn't really casual at all. He was claiming possession, daring Dalton to challenge that claim.

"Didn't trust me, huh, counselor?" Abby teased.

He looked down at her with a slight frown. "I'd trust you with anything I have, Abby," he said softly.

She looked away from that disturbing glance with a nervous smile.

"Dinner is served!" Mrs. McDougal called from the dining room.

All through the delicious meal, Dalton's eyes never left Abby. By the time Mrs. McDougal brought in the homemade apple pie with cream, McCallum was smoldering quietly at the head of the table. His gray eyes met Abby's once, and there was blatant accusation in them, as if Dalton's interest were her fault. In a way, she thought, it probably was. She hadn't actually rejected his subtle overtures. She couldn't. There was something barely begun and still unfinished between them. And even though she'd told herself it was over, even though she'd responded unconditionally to McCallum's passion, a small part of her still responded to Robert Dalton. How much was something she had to find out alone.

When Mrs. McDougal called Grey aside to check with him about menus, Dalton saw his chance and took it.

"Abby, I've got to talk to you," he said urgently. "Have dinner with me tomorrow. Just that, just dinner. Surely you can spare me that much of your time?"

She felt the discomfort like a touch. Her eyes flicked to McCallum, to find him talking to Mrs. McDougal but looking straight at her with a challenging glint to them. The glint decided her. She wasn't his possession, despite his possessive attitude.

"I'll have dinner with you," she said. "We can go straight from the office tomorrow afternoon. I get off at five."

His face lit up. He smiled. "I've missed you."

She'd missed him too. It had been an ache that had almost driven her mad soon after she left Charleston. But, like all aches it had faded with time. Now, seeing him, watching him, she wasn't sure that it had completely gone. That was why she needed time. She needed to be sure.

"Abby's agreed to have dinner with me tomorrow night," Dalton said without preamble after McCallum had let Mrs. McDougal out of the apartment. "I hope you don't mind."

He did. It showed in every rigid line of his face, in the flash of silver eyes that pierced Abby's. "Just bring her home early," McCallum said with a smile she didn't like. "Let's get down to business, shall we?

Abby's working on a manuscript, she can amuse herself."

"I'll say good night, if you don't mind," she told Dalton, giving him her hand. "I like to work in my room, that way I don't disturb Grey."

"Our room, darling," McCallum retorted with a mocking smile. "You shouldn't have any trouble finishing that scene you were working on this afternoon," he added, "now that you've researched it."

She just escaped a livid blush. "Good night," she murmured, flashing a glare at him.

"Surely you can do better than that?" he purred.

She was going to have to kiss him, and in front of Dalton. It was the last straw. Well, two could play his game. She'd give him something to color his dreams.

With a sensuous smile, she moved toward him, standing on tiptoe to reach his disciplined mouth.

"See you later, darling," she whispered sweetly, and her fingers tangled in his dark hair to bring his mouth down over hers. Out of the corner of her eye, she noticed Dalton turning his head discreetly to study the books in the bookcase. Feeling utterly wicked, she pressed her hips hard against Grey's and her tongue teased his mouth before it shot into the warm darkness, tempting him, seducing him. She felt his breath quicken, felt his fingers digging violently into her waist as he suddenly took over. His mouth crushed hers, his tongue taught her sensations she hadn't felt even in the privacy of the study earlier that night. His hands caught her hips and moved them sensuously against his. She'd been bluffing, but he wasn't. He knew all the moves, and to her horror, an anguished little moan tore out of her throat as the ache rose like a river in flood inside her body.

Grey put her away from him suddenly, smiling like a rake. "Sleep well," he murmured.

As if she'd sleep a wink after that, she thought as she wobbled down the hall. Damned arrogant man.

CHAPTER FIVE

How she slept at all after their dinner with Dalton and McCallum's good-night kiss was a minor miracle. But she woke up with a nagging headache and a strange new sense of emptiness. Greyson McCallum had kindled fires in her body that she hadn't dreamed of. It had faintly shocked her to find out how passionately she could respond to a man. She'd never felt that way with Gene. In all honesty, she'd never felt that way with Robert Dalton.

She glanced at the clock beside the bed and suddenly jumped to her feet. Breakfast would be in ten minutes and McCallum wouldn't wait. Her face colored slightly, as she thought about how it was going to be when she looked into those hard gray eyes again. Despite his relentless chiding, he'd been every bit as involved as she was last night. She could still feel the rough sigh of his breath against her mouth, the hardness of his demanding body against every soft, aching inch of hers. In all the long months she'd worked with him, she'd never dreamed there was such an ardent lover under that monumental reserve of his.

She dressed in a two-piece tweed suit with a long-sleeved blouse, all in different shades of brown and beige. The effect, with her long, loosened blond hair, was memorable. She slid her feet into a pair of beige pumps and hurriedly dabbed on some lipstick and powder before she grabbed her purse and went down the hall toward the kitchen.

McCallum was already working his way through an egg and mushroom omelet. The smile Abby had felt surging up to her lips died somewhere in her throat when he looked up. The expression was familiar. It was the one he wore when the district attorney's name was mentioned, or when he, rarely, lost a case. It was accompanied by a black scowl and glittering eyes, and right now Abby was being treated to both.

"You're late," he said shortly. "Go and tell Mrs. McDougal what you want, and be quick. I'm leaving here in exactly ten minutes."

She wanted to tell him where he could go in those ten minutes, but it didn't seem like the best time.

"Yes, your worship," she murmured under her

breath as she went through the door to the kitchen, not waiting to catch his response.

"Ill-tempered as a wet hornet this morning, he is," Mrs. McDougal murmured, muffling a smile when Abby joined her. "He always has three eggs in his omelet—this morning he wanted one. I buttered the toast, and he wanted it plain. The coffee was too strong. Too strong! He's always wanted it twice-boiled, and this morning I made it just a bit weaker than usual!" She shook her head. "If he takes his mean disposition to the office, you will have all the sympathy I can muster."

"Thanks, I'll need it. Just toast for me, Mrs. McDougal," she said with a twinkling smile. "It's hard to enjoy a meal when you're eating in a tiger's cage."

"I'll not argue with that." Mrs. McDougal grinned. "The things love does to a man." She sighed, turning away just in time to miss Abby's flush.

When Abby took her toast back in, McCallum was creaming his second cup of coffee and looking even more impatient than usual. He was wearing a gray pin-striped suit with a charcoal gray vest and a stark white shirt. His tie was a striped one in various shades of silvery gray and blue, and the combination emphasized his dark hair, his tanned complexion. He looked . . . extraordinarily handsome, she thought.

"Is that what you're wearing tonight?" he

growled, glancing at her. "Or is Dalton bringing you here to change?"

She gave him a surprised look over the toast she was nibbling. "I'm wearing this," she said. "I don't need to change just for dinner."

"No? You're sure you wouldn't rather wear that little number you had on last night for him?" he chided.

Just the memory of his hands on her warm, soft body made the blood careen drunkenly through her veins.

She put the rest of her toast down and sipped her coffee. "I'm only having dinner with him, Mr. McCallum," she said tightly.

"That wasn't all you were having with him a year ago," he shot back. His eyes narrowed. "I told you at the beginning that I don't like being made to look like a fool. Dinner, okay. But just be sure you don't end up being dessert. You make one false move with him, and I'll make your life hell. That's a promise."

He didn't have to add that last sentence, she thought miserably. She knew McCallum well enough to have tacked it on all by herself. He didn't make idle threats.

"You're just furious because I wouldn't fall in line and do exactly what you said," she grumbled. "Is that what you expect from your women, McCallum? Blind obedience?"

"Among other things," he replied, and his darkening eyes said more than the words. They traced the soft curves of her breasts until she wanted to scream. "You've got a lot to learn, Miss Summer," he murmured deeply. "But you've got promise."

She let her eyes rest on the half-full cup of black coffee under her cool fingers. "We . . . we agreed that this was going to be just a business arrangement."

That hardened his face. "Did we? Then, by all means, Miss Summer, we'll stick to it." He drained his cup and got up from the chair, leaving her to follow.

He opened the apartment door for her, blocking it for just an instant as he looked down into her troubled eyes. "Are you ashamed of last night, Abby, is that it?" he asked in a low, deep tone.

Her face flushed and she stared down at the carpet. "I'd rather forget last night," she choked.

"Did he make you feel like that?" he asked gently. "Did he make you beg?"

The flush got worse, and her hunted eyes met his. "No fair, counselor," she managed. "I . . . I had a lot to drink . . ."

"You had a sip of brandy," he corrected. "The only thing you were drunk on was passion."

"Damn you!" she cried. She ducked under his arm and almost ran ahead of him down the hall.

Fortunately, the preliminary preparation for the White murder trial kept McCallum busy when they got to the office. Abby lost track of the people who came and went, leaving behind bits and pieces that

McCallum would wind into a case once he got into the courtroom. One of the visitors was his surprise witness, a nervous young brunette who was an eyewitness to the brutal slaying. McCallum had kept that fact close to home so that Clever Hardway, the hard-nosed district attorney, wouldn't get wind of the surprise witness and use her to his own advantage.

While she was still in conference with McCallum, Abby answered the phone and found Hardway breathing down her ear.

"What is he holding back?" he demanded without the courtesy of a greeting—unusual for the very gentlemanly manner he usually presented. "I'm hearing rumors I don't like, Abby. If he throws me any curves in this case, I'll barbecue him in front of God and the jury, I swear it!"

"Now, Mr. Hardway," she began in her best soothing tone, the one that worked ten percent of the time on McCallum, "I'm sure Mr. McCallum has told you everything . . ."

"He's told me everything but the truth," came the heated reply. "I'm sick to my argyle socks of having him introduce surprise witnesses just minutes before the closing arguments!"

Abby chewed delicately on one long, pink nail to keep from giggling. "But surely you'd know . . ." she protested gently.

"How could I know?" he burst out. "He bribes people to keep their mouths shut! He must, there's such a conspiracy of silence around here! You tell him . . . never mind, I'll tell him, put him on the phone."

"I can't do that, Mr. Hardway, he's in conference . . ."

"He's always in conference," came the harried reply. "Or out on a personal emergency. Or eating lunch! It's impossible for any man to run a law practice and be out of the office as much as he is! And he won't return my calls, not once has he ever returned one of my calls!" There was a slow, deliberate sigh on the other end of the line, and when it was over, Hardway's voice sounded calmer. "Tell Mr. McCallum, if you will, that I do *not* intend to be shown up in court on this one. I have done my homework. But if I hear one more rumor about a surprise witness, I will come over there and shake your employer by his ears until he levels with me. And you may quote me when you give him the message. Good-bye, Abby."

She stared at the receiver. A giggle tickled her throat and burst out despite her efforts to control it.

"What's so funny?" Jan asked as she passed the desk.

"Mr. Hardway," she replied, indicating the receiver. "He said that if McCallum brought in a surprise witness this time, he was going to come over and shake him by the ears."

Jan went away laughing. Clever Hardway, while a brilliant prosecuting attorney, was not up to McCallum's size by any stretch of imagination. The D. A. was only five foot six.

When the little brunette left McCallum's office, casting a nervous smile in Abby's direction, it was time for lunch. Abby was in the middle of an especially long petition with descriptions of the exhibits McCallum planned to have entered into evidence in the White trial, so she'd asked Jan to bring her back a sandwich and a soft drink.

McCallum glanced at her as he came through his open door. "Not taking lunch today?" he asked shortly.

She shook her head. "No time."

"So efficient, Miss Summer," he said with biting sarcasm.

"Don't sink your sharp teeth into me, please," she muttered. "I've just been nibbled on by the district attorney and I'm sore all over."

"Hardway called?" His eyebrows shot up. "What did he want?"

"He's hearing rumbles about your surprise witness," she told him.

He stuck his hands into his pockets and a half smile touched his firm mouth. "What kind of rumbles?"

"Rumors." She glanced up at him, still typing while she talked. "He said that if you pull another surprise witness on him, he'll come over here and shake you by the ears."

That broke the black mood he'd been in all morning. He threw back his head and roared. "My God, is he going to use a stepladder?"

She bit back a smile. "He didn't say." She ran out of space on the page and drew the original and carbons out, replacing the carbons neatly on other legal-size sheets. "That reminds me, that luncheon your civic club is giving for Mr. Hardway is next Thursday at noon. It's an appreciation day lunch."

"I don't appreciate him," he shot back, his eyes glittering.

"I don't get the idea that he appreciates you very much, either," she laughed.

"Do I have to take a present? Find me a picture of a horse's—"

"Mr. McCallum!"

He studied her faintly flushed face with amusement. "Point taken." His eyes watched her, sketched her face. "Don't you think you're taking a hell of a risk by going out alone with Dalton?"

"It's only dinner," she protested.

"Is it?"

She looked up into his eyes and found them held, captured. Something intensely personal locked their gazes until her heart went wild inside her. She couldn't move, couldn't speak, she felt as if she were drowning in those deep gray eyes.

"Can he give you what we had last night, Abby?" he asked very quietly. And then, without another word, he turned and walked out the door.

She stared after him with conflicting emotions.

No, Dalton couldn't give her the kind of pleasure McCallum had, it was ridiculous to assume that he could. Because Dalton no longer held her heart, and she was only just beginning to realize it.

It was one minute to five when Robert Dalton walked into the office, his fairness complemented by his expensive blue suit.

"Made it, just," he said with a smile. "Is Grey in?" he added.

"Uh, no, he didn't come back to the office after lunch," she said, and stopped short of admitting how unusual that was. "I'll just be a minute."

Dalton took her to an exclusive restaurant in an even more exclusive shopping center outside the city. It was faintly reminiscent of Charleston, especially when the delicious chilled prawns and spicy cocktail sauce were served. The lobster thermidor was excellent, like the aged white wine Dalton ordered to go with it, along with baked potatoes stuffed with bacon and chives and butter, and flaky homemade croissants. For dessert there was a lemon tart, served with luscious whipped cream, that Abby couldn't refuse.

"I don't know when I've enjoyed anything more," Abby sighed over her coffee, smiling at Dalton over the flower arrangement.

"My pleasure, Abby," he replied. He set his own cup down and stared at her. "How did you manage?" he asked gently, and there was genuine concern in his voice.

She smiled wistfully. "I went to work for McCallum," she explained. "I had very little time for self-pity or regret. He's . . . an unusual man."

He shifted uncomfortably. "I could have shot myself for my own cowardice," he said softly. "It took weeks to get over the look on your face when Liz walked in and I . . . put the blame on you." He grimaced. "It just burst out. Liz held the purse strings. I had money of my own, but all of it was tied up in investments. She could have and still can bankrupt me in a divorce suit. But what I did to you was unforgivable."

"No," she said gently. She reached out and touched his hand lightly. "Not unforgivable. We're all human, Robert."

"When Liz agreed to the separation, I looked for you," he admitted. "But you'd disappeared into thin air."

She laughed. "It was still a one-way street, you know," she told him, her voice soft. "There was no future for us."

He started to speak, but apparently thought better of it, and laughed shortly. "If by that, you mean I'd never have been able to offer you marriage, I suppose that's the truth. But, Abby, neither has McCallum. What kind of future can you expect with him?"

She'd never given that much thought, but like a lot of other new ideas, it rushed in to confound her. A future with McCallum. To live with him and be loved by him, to sit and watch him while he worked into the night, to take care of him when he was sick and have him to hold close to her late in the night. . . .

"I've known Grey for years," he continued quietly. "Any woman who could last more than a few months with him would be unique indeed. Marriage isn't in his vocabulary."

"Yes, I know," she replied quietly. How often had she heard McCallum say that same thing? And it had made her laugh months ago. Now, it made her want to cry.

Dalton saw that look and launched into memories of when they were getting to know each other in Charleston. She found to her amazement that she could look back at them without remorse. It was a closed chapter in her life, and surprisingly it didn't hurt too badly to look at it. It was a little like taking out an old photograph, one of a cherished memory, and revisiting it. There was no pain, only a feeling of mild pleasure.

It was just barely eleven o'clock when Dalton escorted her to the door of McCallum's apartment.

He looked down at her with a sad, wistful expression in his pale blue eyes, and smiled. "It's too late for us, isn't it, Abby?" he asked.

She managed a smile. "I'm afraid so."

He nodded toward the apartment. "Is he good to you?"

"Oh, yes," she lied, remembering how he'd spent the morning growling like a hungry lion.

Dalton nodded. "I hope he realizes what a treasure he has." His pale blue eyes were wistful as they scanned her face. "I'm sorry that I didn't. We could have had something very special, Abby."

She reached up and touched his cheek lightly. "There were good times, you know," she said gently. "I enjoyed being with you. You were kind to me at a time when I desperately needed kindness. I'll never forget that."

He smiled sadly. "Would you mind very much if I kissed you?"

She shook her head, moving closer. He bent and she felt the hard, firm crush of his mouth for the first time in over a year. He brought her closer, deepening the kiss, as if trying to recapture what they'd once had. But now Abby had McCallum's rough ardor for comparison. Against it, Robert Dalton was almost an amateur. Abby felt a very gentle kind of pleasure in his embrace, but it was nothing like the fires McCallum had kindled. The difference was like that between a soothing breeze and a hurricane.

At last, Dalton drew back, frowning slightly at Abby's composed features. He let her go with a world-weary sigh. "You know something, Abby?" he said softly. "I used to think that I could be utterly content if I had enough wealth to satisfy every need and whim. Now, I can do that. And it isn't enough. It will never be enough."

She felt a faint maternal stirring as she saw beneath the calm face, all the way to a deep, lingering emptiness. He wasn't a happy man, she wondered if he'd ever been happy. Some people, and he seemed to be one of them, had an outlook on life which precluded happiness in any form. They expected heartache, and of course it came running.

"Thank you for the evening," she said. She opened the door. "We'll see each other again before you go, I'm sure."

"So we will. But it won't be the same, Abby," he added wistfully. He smiled halfheartedly before he walked away.

The apartment was empty. McCallum wasn't home, and that was odd indeed. Nicky had said that he loved his privacy and didn't like sharing it, but Abby had assumed that he meant his older brother spent a lot of time at home. Now she began to wonder if the reverse wasn't true. Perhaps he was tired of Abby, of having a second person in his home. Perhaps, too, he was out with that bottled redhead. Something uncurled and yawned inside her, something unreasonable that suddenly wanted to start pulling out dyed red hair. Abby shook herself mentally. This was none of her business. McCallum had always had women, and that fact had never bothered her before. She thought of Vinnie Nichols and saw red; a red that had nothing to do with hair. McCallum, with that woman, when he was supposed to be living with Abby!

She tried to work on her novel, but she couldn't concentrate. She paced, she stared at the clock, she watched television programs without seeing them. In desperation, she took a bath. It was midnight, but still no McCallum.

At one o'clock, she went to bed. She had to, or she knew she'd never be able to get up in the morning. But a part of her mind stayed alert, listening for the sound of a key in the door, a telephone call. What if he'd had an accident? She sat straight up in bed. After all, she reasoned, he'd been away from the office since lunch. What if he'd been hit by a car or something and the people at the hospital didn't know who he was? Or worse, what if Clever Hardway had sent the police out to arrest him for withholding evidence? What if the Martians had captured him? What if he'd turned into a puddle of mushroom gravy? With a groan she lay back down again. Lack of sleep was making her hysterical. Of course he was all right. He was just shacked up with that redhead. She rolled over and thumped the pillows violently, burying her hot face in them.

Just before she finally fell asleep, she had a deliciously satisfying fantasy in which McCallum broke his arm and Abby nursed him back to health after which he confessed his passionate love for her. The thought caused a vivid dream from which she woke in a flushed daze.

* * *

The alarm clock was buzzing noisily when she opened her eyes and flung out a drowsy hand to shut it off. She felt as if she'd hardly slept at all, and the first thought she had was that McCallum might not have come home at all.

She felt a kindling rage like nothing she'd experienced before as she jumped out of bed, not even pausing long enough to sling on a robe as she padded over the carpet to the door and opened it angrily. Down the hall in the kitchen, there were rattling sounds and soft humming, which meant that Mrs. McDougal was already getting breakfast. Was McCallum home or not?

Abby went across the hall to the master bedroom and opened the door with a savage jerk. *Philandering, miserable* . . . She froze in the doorway. McCallum was home all right. Her wide eyes locked onto his big, masculine body sprawled completely naked and sound asleep on the cover of the bed.

CHAPTER SIX

It certainly wasn't the first time Abby had seen a man without clothes. But her memory of Gene's lean pale body was no match for what she saw on the silky chocolate bedspread in front of her stunned eyes.

McCallum was solid muscle, from the tips of his toes all the way up, broad hair-roughened thighs, lean hips, massive hairy chest, powerful arms . . . he was tan all over too, as if he spent his vacations sunbathing in the nude on those French beaches he favored. If a man could be called beautiful, he was; a candidate for a centerfold if ever there was one.

After a minute, she managed to drag her eyes away from his blatant masculinity and turned to leave the room. On her way out, his hastily discarded shirt caught her eye. It was lying on top of his trousers in a chair, its spotless white front smeared from the second button to the collar with pale orange lipstick. That shade was instantly recognizable to Abby. She'd noticed distastefully how caked Vinnie Nichols's wide mouth always was with it.

So that was where he'd been, she thought venomously. She gave his sleeping body one last, furious glance before she closed the door on the sight of him.

She was more composed when she went to have breakfast, wearing a becoming blue-green dress that was high collared and beautifully pleated from shoulder to waist. It flattered her small waist and her firm, high breasts. She set it off with black slingback shoes and a matching leather purse. And her green eyes were greener than burning emeralds under the frown she couldn't help.

"I'll have to go and wake Mr. McCallum," Mrs. McDougal sighed, noticing the time. "Or he'll never get to work on time."

"Uh, you needn't bother," Abby said quickly, remembering the sight of him. "He had a late night last night, and the sleep will do him good." She grinned at the thought of her punctual employer arriving late; it would shock old George, and Jan would giggle. . . . She flushed, remembering what they were sure to think, and it wouldn't be only McCallum they'd be giggling at. But she couldn't wake him up—he'd still been out when she dropped off around one thirty, which meant he'd surely only had a few hours of sleep. She grimaced. There was nothing to do but let him sleep. She wondered why he hadn't just spent the night with Vinnie. Perhaps he'd been hoping that Abby would be sitting in the apartment, getting more jealous by the minute. And, of course, she had. But McCallum wasn't going to have the satisfaction of knowing that. No, sir.

"Are you sure he won't awaken roaring around and mad enough to fire me?" Mrs. McDougal laughed. "Oh, he's got a temper on him, that one."

"Just speak in a soft voice, don't show fear, and don't make any sudden moves," Abby instructed. "It works every time."

Mrs. McDougal watched the younger woman finish half a piece of toast and wash it down with black coffee. "Now that's a masterly bit of advice. May I ask where you learned it?"

Abby grinned at her. "I read an article once about what to do if you were ever confronted with an attack dog."

Mrs. McDougal went back into the kitchen, laughing so hard that tears streamed down her cheeks.

Abby's bus was five minutes late, and when she walked into the office, Jan was sitting on the edge of Abby's desk chewing a fingernail into shreds.

"Oh, thank goodness you're here!" the petite blonde sighed. "Abby, where's Mr. McCallum?" she added, staring around her friend as if she might be concealing the attorney behind her.

"At home asleep," Abby said shortly. "Why?"

Jan started to say something, but closed her mouth quickly at the expression on the taller woman's face. "It's that divorce case Jerry was handling," she explained. "He's got one and Mr. McCallum has one he's handling as a favor to one of his friends, remember?"

"How could I forget?" Abby groaned. "That wailing woman has caused me grief in the middle of preparations for that murder trial. I've had to wipe away tears and listen to her on the phone, and track down McCallum at all hours of the day . . . anyway, what's wrong?"

Jan looked toward the ceiling. "Jerry called and left word for McCallum's client to be at the courthouse in the city at 9:30 A.M. and told his client to be in Addison at the same time today."

"So? You did know that the case had to be tried in the woman's county of residence?" Abby murmured absently as she uncovered her typewriter calmly.

"That's just the point." She sighed miserably. "Oh, Abby, Jerry called the wrong number. *Jerry's* client lives in this county; *she's* not supposed to be in Addison at 9:30 A.M. today, McCallum's client is. McCallum will chew his ears off—but right now, what do I do? McCallum's supposed to handle that case, and Jerry's on his way to court in the city, and . . ."

"Sit down," Abby said gently, helping Jan into the chair behind the uncovered typewriter. "Take two deep breaths. Then type these letters for me—one is about a deposition McCallum wants taken in the White case, the other is to the legal organ to explain a notice of incorporation for a merger he's entering into with Robert Dalton. You take care of that. And I will save Jerry's life."

Jan smiled. "Now I know what true friendship is."

Abby smiled back. She opened the door to McCallum's office. "Now, let's see, what am I going to ask Jerry for in return? The keys to his car, his stereo, his credit card. . . ."

It took all of thirty minutes, but Abby caught Jerry in time to have him send the woman McCallum was representing to Addison. At the same time, she called the clerk of court's office in Addison and had Jerry's client notified of the mix-up. Then she reached an attorney in Addison who was an old partner in the firm Jerry Smith had previously been associated with and sweet-talked him into substituting for McCallum. She hoped she'd be forgiven for telling the unsuspecting substitute that her absent boss was nursing a sudden illness. It sounded better than telling people he'd collapsed after a drunken orgy.

McCallum didn't come into the office until after

eleven o'clock. He looked drawn under his scowl, and there were lines of fatigue carved into his rigid face. He glared at Abby, standing over her desk like a phantom in his black suit. She couldn't help thinking how the shade matched his expression.

"Well?" he asked silkily. "You told McDougal to let me sleep, didn't you? Don't you know I had a damned court case in Addison at nine thirty?"

"All taken care of," she said distantly. "James Davis is handling it for you. I cleared the calendar for this morning and I've caught up the paperwork and the correspondence."

"Why the hell didn't you wake me up?" he asked shortly.

She lifted her eyebrows haughtily. "After your wild, mad night with your even wilder artist friend? God forbid."

He stared at her unblinkingly. "What makes you think I was with Vinnie?"

"The lipstick smeared all over your . . ." She stopped short, knowing already that the admission had told him everything.

He lifted an eyebrow and began to chuckle softly at the expression on her face. "Got an anatomy lesson, did you?"

She really flushed then, and he chuckled wickedly. "Oh, hush," she snapped. "You might have had the decency to put on a pair of pajamas."

"I don't wear pajamas, Abby," he remarked dryly. "They only get in the way."

She avoided his pointed gaze. For a man who'd walked in looking ready to do murder, his mood had improved with incredible speed.

"You're supposed to meet Bill Sellers for lunch today at twelve at the Marble Room," she said, biting back a comment.

"Did you sit up and wait for me?" he chided.

"Did you expect me to?" she countered, eyes blazing. "It's none of my business if you want to spend your evenings getting drunk and getting . . ."

He started laughing and couldn't seem to stop. Abby sat and seethed, picturing a noose around his thick neck.

"I think you and I had better have a nice long talk after work today," he said finally. "We need to clear up a few things."

"Are you sure your poor throbbing head will stand it?" she taunted.

He cocked an eyebrow. "I don't have a hangover," he replied with a faint smile. "Were you hoping to spend the rest of the day slamming doors and making noise? Sorry to spoil your fun."

"You didn't," she said shortly. "Robert and I had a lovely evening."

"Did you?" He lifted his head and stared down his arrogant nose at her.

"A lovely evening," she repeated with a stage sigh and a dreamy smile.

"By that," he said with a cool smile, "I assume

that you didn't have too much trouble helping the poor old doddering fellow in and out of cars?"

She picked up a paperweight and stared at him with furious eyes.

"It would only break," he informed her as he went sauntering into his office and closed the door.

Abby's temper didn't improve, but McCallum's certainly did. He was like a lamb around the office for the rest of the day. Not once did he yell or rake Abby over the coals for not getting a letter typed fast enough. He didn't complain about Jan's coffee or even give Jerry hell about the mix-up that morning. He seemed like a man with happy secrets—which made Abby all the madder. She just knew that he was remembering the night with Vinnie!

Abby was almost relieved when five o'clock came. Once they got back to the apartment, she could lock herself in her room and write and just ignore the infuriating man.

But when she was comfortably seated in McCallum's sleek black Porsche, she suddenly realized that he wasn't driving in the direction of his apartment. He seemed to be heading out of town.

"Where are we going?" she asked, sitting up straight.

He took a long draw from his cigarette and his eyes slid toward her for just a minute. "To spend the night with Mother and Nick," he said. "Collette's going to be there."

"Wait a minute," she said quickly. "What do you mean spend the night? And what has Collette got to do with it?"

"You seem to think I've got the wrong impression of her, don't you?" he chided. "Well, this is my chance to see what she's really like."

"I suppose so. But there aren't that many bedrooms even though it's a big house . . ." she frowned.

"We'll worry about that later," he said. He grinned at her. "Come on, Abby, wouldn't you like a brisk morning ride in the woods? Peace and quiet, leaves rustling, mist on the river . . ."

"Well . . ." She felt herself weakening.

"Mother's making peach cobbler for dessert," he added.

"Oh, I'll go without another argument," she burst out, already tasting the delicacy that was her favorite; and nobody made it like Mandy McCallum. The sandwich she'd had at lunch had already left, and her stomach was feeling dreadfully empty.

"Hungry?" he teased.

"Terribly," she admitted. Her eyes flirted with him. "My boss is a slave driver. He's terrible to me."

"I am? My God, let me make amends right now!" He pulled the car off onto the side of the little-traveled county road and left it idling with the brake on. Before Abby knew what was happening, he'd undone her seat belt and jerked her out of her bucket seat and into his lap.

"But, Grey . . . !" she burst out.

"Hush, baby," he whispered against her mouth. "Just . . . hush."

His hard mouth bit at hers in brief, searing kisses that very quickly kindled the fires he'd lit once before. Her lips softened and parted, her fingers lifted to tangle in his thick, dark hair and pull his head even closer.

She felt his fingers lift under one high, firm breast and take its delicate weight while his thumb nudged the taut nipple in a slow, maddening motion.

She moaned involuntarily against his mouth and felt him smile.

"More?" he whispered sensuously. He opened the buttons at the front of her dress, his hand sliding up to the front catch of the lacy bra, flicking it open with the ease of long practice. She gasped as his fingers touched and teased the soft bareness of her body and made it writhe with the force of the pleasure. She buried her hot face in his throat, her nails digging into the soft fabric of his suit.

His hard lips brushed over her forehead, her closed eyes. "Look at me, honey," he whispered.

Her eyes slid open lazily, wide and dark green and misty with emotion, framed by disheveled blond hair that was more becoming than any hard-done coiffure.

"You're very good at this," she managed in a voice that shook.

"And you're very lovely," he said gently. His fingers moved, fastening the catch on her bra, then buttoning the front of her dress. "Didn't your husband even get around to teaching you the basics?" he asked quietly.

She shook her head. "He assumed that I already knew them." She smiled wistfully. "I didn't know anything except what I'd read and the little my parents taught me. I went to strict schools and I had an even stricter upbringing. The first time was a nightmare. The rest of my marriage was a little more bearable, I guess. Gene wasn't anybody's idea of the world's greatest lover. Perhaps he just didn't want me enough." She looked up at him briefly, her face flushing just a little. "I could never talk to him the way I can talk to you. I always thought I would never really enjoy making love."

She expected him to smile at that, but he didn't. He looked deeply somber. "But we know differently now, don't we?"

She dropped her eyes to his collar, stained with her lipstick. "You're smudged," she murmured. "And neither of us has a change of clothes to go riding in."

"I keep some clothes at the house." He grinned. "You can't wear mine, I don't imagine, but I'll bet you could wear a pair of Nick's jeans and one of his sweaters."

She couldn't argue with that, she was about Nick's build except for a few additional bulges. "I'd like to go riding with you," she admitted.

He drew a deep, slow breath, and something flared up in his silver eyes. "Honey, there are one hell of a lot of things I'd like to do with you. More than I ever realized . . ." He put her back into her own seat. "We'd better get down the road. I'm too old to let myself get arrested for public indecency—added to which," he murmured with a wicked smile, "Jerry would enjoy defending me too much."

She laughed with him. The idea kept her smiling all the way to the house.

Mandy McCallum met them at the door, all her misgivings showing in her face. "Oh, Grey, you aren't going to cause trouble, are you?" she asked softly. "It's Nicky's birthday in two days, and if you have a fight with him . . ."

"I'm not going to have a fight with him," McCallum said with a smile. He bent and kissed the older woman's cheek. "Say hello to Abby and stop worrying."

"Hello, Abby," she said obediently. "I made you a peach cobbler, did Grey tell you?"

"Yes," Abby agreed. Impulsively, she kissed Mandy, too. "You're an angel."

"There you are!" Nick called from the doorway. He came through it in a rush, dragging a shy little creature with short dark hair and huge, shining eyes behind him. "Grey, Abby, this is Collette."

McCallum stared down at the little Dresden-china doll, and all the hard lines seemed to go out of his face. "Hello, Collette," he said in his kindest voice. "You're as lovely as Nick told me you were," he added.

The French girl smiled shyly and her huge brown eyes sparkled as they briefly averted to Nick. "Thank you, Monsieur Grey," she said. "I also have heard much of you. I am glad that we meet at last." She edged closer to Nick and clung to his arm like a lifeline.

Mandy breathed a visible sigh of relief. "There's nothing better for my nerves than having my family all together at once," she muttered as she led the way inside.

Mandy had outdone herself. There was chicken-fried steak and gravy, homemade yeast rolls, a tossed salad, mashed potatoes, asparagus with a cheese sauce—and that delicious cobbler for dessert. Abby felt like a stuffed bird as she finished the last morsel of the cobbler in her saucer.

"I'll put the rest of it in the refrigerator, Abby," Mandy told her. "And if you get up before Nicky does, you can have it."

"Peach cobbler for breakfast?" McCallum burst out, gaping at Abby.

She sat up straighter. "There's nothing wrong with peach cobbler for breakfast. I've seen you eat steak," she reminded him.

"At least steak is civilized," he retorted.

"Not the way you eat it, it isn't," she giggled. "Your steaks try to run for it when they see you coming."

"Just like the witnesses the D. A. brings in,"

Nicky chuckled. "Grey's a lawyer," he reminded Collette.

"As you told me," the French girl smiled. "You must be very smart, Monsieur, to carry so much knowledge of the law around in your head."

"You flatter me," McCallum replied gently. "What do you do, Collette?"

"Do?" She glanced at Nicky. "Oh, a job, you mean? I have helped my father with the winery, so that someday I will earn the care of the vineyard when my father has retired. I am the only child, you see; they will be my responsibility, all the vines."

"Your father has a vineyard?" McCallum asked casually—too casually, as he leaned back in his chair and lit a cigarette.

Nicky chuckled. "Have you ever heard of d'Anece wines?"

McCallum's eyebrows shot up. "Who hasn't? They're internationally known for excellence."

"Collette's father is Raoul d'Anece."

It only took the older man an instant to recover. "You might have told me that at the beginning, little brother," he said with a smile that covered a vein of suppressed temper.

"We all need a few surprises to keep our mundane lives percolating, Grey," he replied, grinning merrily.

McCallum blew out a thin cloud of smoke and couldn't hold back a chuckle. "That's one up for you," he admitted. "Now, how about a brandy and let's talk over some business."

"You've got an account for me?" Nick asked eagerly.

"That depends on how good you are at your job."

"Oh, Nicky is the best," Collette assured McCallum, and she gazed up at Nick with worshipful eyes. "Truly."

Abby saw the way Nick looked back at the girl, and she was glad things were working out. It looked as if McCallum's younger brother had finally found something he was willing to fight for.

McCallum and Nick talked business for most of the night, discussing campaigns, publicity, and finance in terms that boggled Abby's mind. She sat on the sidelines with Mandy and Collette, sharing a new *Harper's Bazaar* while they discussed the latest fashions. Collette was knowledgeable about the trends, pointing out the latest styles that had caught on in Europe. Collette and Mandy seemed to get along well, too, which was a good thing if that look between Nick and the younger woman was anything to go by.

Abby's eyes, meanwhile, wandered restlessly over McCallum. He had shed his suit coat and vest and had rolled up his sleeves. Several of the buttons on his shirt were unfastened down the front, and every time he moved, the thin fabric strained sensuously over the broad muscles of his chest. She remembered achingly the feel and touch and taste of him, the way he'd looked stretched out so blatantly masculine on his bed. Her pulse hopscotched wildly when he looked up and caught that intense appraisal. He didn't smile, and the tension between them was suddenly tangible.

It was after eleven when the discussion broke up. Nicky had to drive Collette back to her hotel in town, and Abby admitted reluctantly that she was tired, too. McCallum grinned wickedly at the admission, and Abby instantly regretted the slip. Now he'd know for certain that she'd waited up half the night for him.

Mandy walked upstairs with Abby while Grey locked up and turned out most of the lights, leaving the porch light on for Nick.

"I've put you both in the guest bedroom," Mandy said. "If Nicky weren't here, you could have his room, but . . ."

"No problem," McCallum said, coming upstairs behind them. "Abby and I are used to sharing. Aren't we, honey?"

Abby flushed. "Uh, supper was delicious," she told Mandy. "Thank you for having me."

"You're very welcome, love," Mandy smiled. She hugged Abby in the hall. "You'll probably leave before I get up in the morning, so come back soon. You're always welcome, even without Greyson."

"Thank you, I'll remember that," Abby promised.

McCallum opened the bedroom door and stood

aside to let Abby go in first. The focal point was the huge double bed in the center of the room, decorated in blue and white patterns with a canopy and wispy curtains. It was all French Provincial, and Abby couldn't help but grin at the idea of as masculine a man as McCallum in that bed.

She peeked up at him. "A little . . . feminine, isn't it?"

He cocked an eyebrow. "A little. No loud protest, Abby?"

She shook her head. "It's a big bed."

"And neither of us has pajamas."

"I intend to do the decent thing and keep my slip on, thanks," she said with theatrical hauteur. "And if you were any kind of a gentleman, you'd wear your shorts."

"Now, what makes you think I'm any kind of a gentleman?" he asked amusedly.

She blinked. Now there was a question. She put her purse on the dresser. "Uh, if you don't mind, I'd like to go ahead and take my bath."

"Through there," he indicated a door. "It's a sunken tub with a heated whirlpool," he added. "Just the thing to relax tension."

"Thank you." She went into the bathroom, closing the door behind her, and found a plush washcloth and towel that matched the burgundy decor. The sunken tub was enormous, almost filling the room, almost big enough to swim in. Abby stripped down quickly after she'd filled it with water and activated the whirlpool unit. As an afterthought, she filled it with bubble bath as well, sending up a cloud of delicious fragrance into the air.

She sank down into the swirling warmth of the water with a huge sigh, her hair loosely pinned atop her head to keep it dry. She closed her eyes and let her tired muscles relax. The whirlpool was just the thing to chase away tension. And wondering how she was going to manage a night in bed with McCallum without screaming from pure frustration was anybody's guess. She was viewing the situation with a jumble of emotions. A part of her wanted more than sleep. Another part was uneasy about that kind of commitment. What she felt for McCallum had grown from an uneasy friendship to a steaming inferno of desire; but not an altogether physical one. While she did want him desperately, she admitted to herself for the first time that she wanted more than a night in his arms. She wanted much more than that.

While she was trying to work out her emotions, she heard the door open. With shocked green eyes she appraised McCallum as he walked in, stark naked, and found himself a washcloth and towel.

She couldn't even get out a question. Her eyes were helplessly riveted to that muscular, tanned body as he got his electric razor from the cabinet and began to shave.

"I'm taking a bath," she said in a squeaky voice.

He glanced at her with an amused smile, noticing

the line of soap bubbles that barely covered her creamy breasts. "So I see. Do you like the whirlpool?" he asked over the combined hums of the razor and the whirlpool unit.

"Oh, yes, I . . . I like it very much, thanks." Well, if he could be nonchalant about it, she could, too. They were both adults. She'd been married, she wasn't naive.

Her fascinated eyes ran up his muscular legs, over his slim hips and broad, heavy shoulders. He was so deliciously masculine, it was all she could do not to climb out of the tub and run her hands over him. She'd never wanted to touch Gene like that, but she'd have given a week's salary just to caress McCallum's smooth, bronzed skin.

"You were right about Collette," he admitted wryly. "But, for future reference, I'm not usually wrong about people. She threw me a curve."

"Naturally. You aren't used to naive little things," she teased.

He lifted an eyebrow at her. "No? I've had you around long enough that I should be."

"I'm not naive."

"About sex, you most certainly are. Delightfully naive," he added sensuously, before she could take offense.

She dabbed at her face with the soapy cloth for something to do. She felt completely out of her element.

"No comment?" he teased. He finished with the

razor and put it back in the cabinet, pausing to splash after-shave on his smooth cheeks. "Don't tell me you're shy?" he chided as he turned around.

She couldn't help the blush. It was simply unavoidable. She dropped her eyes to the washcloth. "I'm not shy at all," she said bravely.

He laughed deeply. "Then why won't you look at me?"

"I'm bathing," she ground out.

"Which does sound like a good idea." And while she was still trying to figure that one out, he picked up his washcloth and towel, threw the latter onto a vanity chair beside the tub, and climbed down into the soap bubbles beside Abby.

CHAPTER SEVEN

Abby's face managed to capture shock, outrage, and fascination in one expression as McCallum slid down into the water right beside her, the soap bubbles catching in the thick mat of hair across his broad chest.

He sighed deeply. "God, that feels good. I've thought about having one of these installed in the apartment, but somehow I never got around to it. Just the thing after a rough day, isn't it, Abby?"

"It's very nice," she agreed. His shoulder was touching hers, and she felt shock waves all the way to her toes, ripples of sweet sensation.

"Soap?"

She handed it to him. "Do you think Nicky is

serious about Collette?" she asked with a valiant effort at nonchalance.

"I think it's a definite possibility," he admitted. He lathered his arms and his chest, and Abby watched him with a dull ache inside her tense body.

He glanced at her and lifted an eyebrow. "Ever fancied yourself as a geisha?" he teased. "How about doing my back?"

He handed her the soapy cloth and turned so that she could reach the muscles, silky with water and dotted with soap bubbles.

She took it and began to smooth it over his darkly tanned skin. She ached to be closer, to touch him without the cloth between her fingers and his hard-muscled body.

While she was trying to stifle the growing hunger, he turned around and saw that look in her eyes before she could erase it.

His chest rose and fell heavily while they looked at each other for a long moment. Then, wordlessly, he took the cloth out of her hand and tossed it into the water. His hands caught hers and lifted them to his soapy chest, moving them slowly, sensuously against it until she got the idea and began to explore his warm torso without any further coaxing.

He smelled of soap and after-shave, and Abby thought there'd never been such a sensuous man in the whole of her life. Her hands moved down his rib cage, to his flat stomach, hesitating, fluttering, when they reached it.

Gently, he guided her hands down even further, and she looked up at him as she touched him, read the pleasure in his darkening eyes that slowly closed, even as she felt the tiny tremor run through his massive body.

She inched toward him, sliding her hands delicately over his broad shoulders until the tips of her breasts were touching his chest. Her lips were parted, her breath coming unsteadily and fast, like his. She leaned forward and brushed her lips softly across his, drawing them back and forth in a whisper of a kiss as she moved again, letting her soft breasts crush down against his slick, hair-covered chest.

He was letting her take the initiative, letting her have all the time she needed, and he seemed to be enjoying it—more than enjoying it if the expression on his broad face was anything to go by. Leaning back, with his glittering eyes like slits under his heavy brows, he watched patiently every move she made. The only indication of emotion under that calm exterior was the thunderous pounding of his heart against her breasts.

"Enjoying yourself, little one?" he asked deeply, his voice as sensuous as a caress.

"I . . . I'd enjoy it more if you'd help me," she whispered against his mouth.

"Help you how?" he whispered. His hands moved then, to slide the length of her spine and back up again. "Like this? Or . . . like this . . ." They moved around her, and he eased her gently back so that his hands could swallow her taut breasts. His fingers caressed them gently, probing, stroking, until she moaned softly.

He eased her across him and one big hand arched her back. He bent to the taut nipples exposed by the motion and took first one, then the other, into his mouth to tease and caress them with his lips, his tongue, his teeth.

Abby's nails bit into his shoulder. She sighed with the pleasure. As his lips slid over her breasts and down to her flat stomach, she bit back a cry.

"For God's sake . . ." he gasped.

He stood up, taking her with him, and riveted her trembling body to the full, hard length of his. His mouth ground down into hers, his tongue thrusting hungrily into her soft mouth, his arms grinding her into him, telling her without words that he had to have more than this.

He broke off the kiss after a moment and reached for his towel. Without another word, he dried every aching inch of her, slowly, the movements of his hands a caress that enveloped her in a blind kind of pleasure. When he was through, he handed the towel to her and stood watching patiently while she did the same for him, her eyes openly adoring him as she dried him from head to toe.

He took the towel away from her, tossed it onto the floor. He lifted her gently in his arms and carried her through the bathroom into the bedroom, laying her down on the blue patterned coverlet of the bed.

She watched as he eased down beside her, so hungry for him that she trembled from head to toe. All she wanted out of life at that moment was to please him, to give him a kind of pleasure he'd never find with anyone else. She wanted him more than life itself.

"I'll take care of you," he whispered as his head bent to her breasts.

She couldn't even answer him. She lay drowning in pleasure as his lips traveled lazily over every soft, sweet inch of her. She alternately moaned and sighed, biting on her lips to keep from crying out loud as he brought her to a crest of sensation that had her writhing like a wild thing.

She felt his broad, hard thighs parting hers, easing between them, and her arms reached up to draw the full weight of his warm, bare chest down over hers, the sensation of skin against skin unbearably sweet. She looked straight up into his eyes, watching him helplessly, as his body merged gently, completely with hers.

She gasped, clinging, a wild little cry escaping her throat even as she stifled it.

"Mother and Nick sleep on the other side of the house," he said in a tight, rough whisper. "There's no one to hear you except me, sweetheart. And, God, Abby, I love the sound of you . . . !"

He took her mouth then, and she arched upward to meet the hungry, hard thrust of his body, her last sane thought that the lights were still on, and she hadn't even cared. Then she began to feel the first stirrings of a wild, savage sweetness that took her complete concentration as she reached, and reached and reached to try to catch it. . . .

She nestled close into McCallum's big arms, damp with perspiration, trembling softly with fulfillment, her moist cheek pressed to the hair-roughened, padded muscles of his chest.

His big hand smoothed her hair tenderly while he smoked, as contented as a jungle cat.

She vaguely remembered murmuring close to his ear that she loved him, as the pleasure washed over her like a thunderous breaking wave. She couldn't remember if he'd acknowledged her words, sounds that may have been unintelligible to him. But she knew now that it was the truth, not part of the incredible passion they'd shared. She loved him.

"I meant to take longer than that," he murmured drowsily.

She smiled shyly. "I don't think I'd have survived if you had," she whispered.

He shifted to look down at her. She'd never seen that particular expression in the silver eyes that traced, deliberately, every exposed inch of her body before they came back to her eyes. "Sweet delight," he said in an uncommonly soft tone, "did I please you?"

"I hope I pleased you," she countered. She nuzzled close and let her eyelids fall.

"Couldn't you tell, honey?" he teased gently.

She smiled. "I hoped."

"Want to go riding with me in the morning?" he murmured.

"Ummmhmmm," she murmured drowsily.

"I'll set the clock. Good night, sweet."

"Good night, Grey," she whispered through a smile.

The last thing she remembered was Grey pulling the covers over them and fitting his body around the shape of hers as she curled on her side and sank into a sweet, dark oblivion.

She woke up all at once, blinking against the daylight filtering in the gauzy curtains. She sat up, and as the covers fell to her waist, she realized that she wasn't wearing a gown—or anything else. Then memory flooded back and she flushed to her collarbone. She'd never meant to let that happen, but the discovery that she loved him had been too much. She'd never known that two people could give and get so much, could please each other in ways that bordered on euphoria. She was faintly embarrassed at the things she'd whispered so feverishly, at the things Grey had whispered back. . . .

She got out of bed and noticed the note on the other pillow. "If you're up by six, I'll be at the breakfast table," it read, and he was hers, Grey. She smiled, reading it a second time, and a third. Perhaps he did care, just a little. He wanted her at least, and that was something. If only Robert Dalton's words hadn't come back to haunt her. McCallum's women only lasted a few months, he'd said. That was so, but Abby wanted far more than a few months. Or even a few years. She wanted the rest of her life with him.

She took a quick bath, trying not to remember what had happened in the tub last night, and dressed in the jeans and sweater that Nick had lent her early last night before she came to bed. They were a little tight, but they felt good, and the shamrock green sweater brought out the vividness of her eyes. She tossed back her hair with the brush, ignored makeup, and rushed down the stairs to the breakfast nook.

McCallum was just setting a platter of eggs and bacon on the table. He looked up as she walked into the room. She stood still in the doorway uncertainly. His face gave nothing away, and she wondered if giving in to him had been the biggest mistake of her life. What if he thought she was cheap, that she was easy? Or even worse, what if that one encounter had wiped out his hunger for her, and he'd never touch her again?

CHAPTER EIGHT

His narrow eyes slid up and down her and suddenly he smiled. It was like daylight breaking on the horizon. All Abby's worries went up in smoke.

"I hope you like eggs and bacon and mushrooms in a messy omelet," he murmured with dry humor. "Because this is the only way I can fix them. The coffee's much better," he promised.

"I don't think I'd notice if it was mud," she admitted with a shy smile.

He put the platter down and moved quickly toward her, to jerk her body against his and kiss her with a warm, slow passion that the night hadn't apparently made a dent in. She felt the hunger in his mouth even as he drew her hips hard against his and told her without words how much he wanted her.

Her arms around his waist, she answered the kiss with a ready response that was new. As new as the look on McCallum's broad face when he lifted his head and her lips clung unashamedly.

"I thought I'd dreamed it until I woke up and found you sound asleep in my arms," he murmured quietly. "It took every ounce of willpower I had to leave you like that. I wanted to kiss you awake and start all over again."

She stood on tiptoe to kiss him, her lips soft and loving. "It was the loveliest dream I've ever had."

"Yes," he said. His voice was deep, his face solemn. He held her close for just an instant before he turned her loose and guided her to the seat beside his.

"Do you often cook breakfast when you're home?" she asked when he'd seated her and himself.

He handed her the platter while he poured the coffee into his mother's thin rose-patterned china cups. "Only when I'm entertaining a lady."

Her eyes jerked up, wounded.

"Abby," he breathed. "I've never brought a woman here before."

She felt embarrassed at letting him see how much it had mattered. She tried to laugh it off. "Oh, I see."

He reached over and covered her hand with his. "Would you like to hear a confession?" he asked gently. "I wasn't with Vinnie—well, I was, but not in the way you thought. She had a few drinks too many and called me to take her home from a party. I put her to bed, but I didn't climb in with her."

"You don't owe me any explanations," she murmured.

"Does that mean you aren't going to admit that you were jealous, Abby?" he murmured with a grin.

She smiled at him over her coffee cup. "That's exactly what it means, counselor."

Later, riding contentedly alongside him in the deep woods that bordered the McCallum property, Abby thought that she'd never seen him quite as relaxed or carefree as he seemed now. The familiar scowl was gone. The lines in his broad face had relaxed. And she felt a new intimacy with him that was devastating.

He caught her looking at him and smiled. "Having fun?" he asked.

"I love this," she admitted. She patted the roan's mane as it paced McCallum's big black gelding. "I used to ride when I was a little girl. One of Dad's friends owned some stables near our house. I got to ride whenever I felt like it."

"What are your parents like?" he asked.

She laughed. "Sunshine," she said without thinking. "I grew up with love and laughter, and I can only remember one honest argument that ended with Dad carrying Mother off to bed." She shook back her long hair delightedly. "They love each other terribly."

"Is your father retired now?"

She nodded. "Yes. As I told you, Mom and Dad

are living in Panama City. He keeps busy. He's much too active a man to sit back and grow flowers."

He glanced at her. "I noticed quite a few pots of them at your apartment."

"I like flowers," she said defensively.

He smiled. "I'll admit to an occasional urge to help Mother hoe the garden."

"Grey, what about Nicky and Collette?" she asked after a minute.

He drew in a deep breath and reined in long enough to light a cigarette. "I've done some thinking about that," he told her. "Perhaps I have infringed on Nick's territory a little. It's hard to admit to myself that he's a man now. I spent a lot of years helping Mother raise him. It's not easy, letting go."

She studied his hard face. "I know. It wasn't easy for me when my parents moved away. I still see them, of course, but it's not like having them a few miles away."

"I promised to fly you down there. I'll do it, the minute I get through with this case."

She smiled. "A few days in the sun wouldn't hurt you," she said. "You work too hard."

"It's been a habit with me," he admitted. His eyes clouded. "I'll never forget the way it used to be, Abby. Poverty leaves its mark. That, and my father's death, were bitter pills to swallow. Sometimes I work myself into a stupor just so that I won't have to think, to remember."

Abby had a feeling that he'd never told that to

another living soul, not even his mother, and she felt warm and close to him.

"Come on," he said suddenly, irritation in his deep voice, "I'll show you the mist rising from the river. It's a sight you won't forget in a hurry."

He led the way and after a few minutes Abby could hear the gurgling sound of the river running lazily between its banks. McCallum reined in and dismounted at the side of a towering oak tree, the roots of which extended down into the river and were partially exposed on one side. He reached up for Abby, and deliberately let her body slide down his as he levered her to the ground.

"Mmmmm," he chuckled, "I like the way you feel. God, you're soft."

"You're not," she teased. She looked up at him for a long moment; just long enough for the hunger between them to kindle again.

His fingers tugged at the buttons of his brown shirt, not stopping until it was open all the way down the front over his broad chest. With a sensuous smile he drew Abby to him.

"What are you wearing under this?" he asked as his fingers tugged at the garment's hem idly.

"Not a thing, Grey," she whispered. Without stopping to think, she reached down and pulled it up over her firm, high breasts just before she flattened them against the warmth of his bare chest by moving forward. She drew them lazily back and forth against him and drew in her breath sharply at the remembered sensations it triggered.

McCallum's hands went down to her hips and lifted her gently, sensuously against the sudden hardness of his thighs, watching her face as the contact stiffened her body.

His eyes slid sideways to a couple of pine trees several yards away where pine straw covered the ground. "I don't know how comfortable this is going to be," he whispered, lifting her suddenly in his arms, "but at least we won't have to worry about interruptions this far from the house."

She drew his mouth onto hers and kissed him slowly, sweetly. He spread out his brown shirt and her sweater and then lay her down on the pine straw, her arms coaxing him down with her.

He moved, covering her trembling body with his so that every inch of them touched. His mouth opened, his tongue darted sharply into her mouth, again and again in a rhythm that matched the aching movements of his hard, heavy body on hers. Her nails dug into his hips and she gasped as the pressure increased the ache inside her until it was almost unbearable.

"I need you," she whispered, her voice shaking. "Please, Grey, oh, please, please . . . !"

"I need you just as much," he ground out, breathing harshly. His hand went between them to the zipper on her jeans. He was already easing it down when a new sound made its way to their feverish minds. It wasn't the soft creak of the trees, or the murmur of the river. It was the sound of horses' hooves and laughing conversation.

McCallum's head jerked up while he listened, and a harsh, explicit word broke from his tight lips as he lifted his body away from Abby's and got to his feet.

"Nick! Of all the damned times to go riding," he muttered, yanking on his shirt. "By God, I'll kill him . . . !"

Abby got up, shaking, hastily picked up the sweater and quickly pulled it over her head. She pressed herself into McCallum's arms and moved close. "Hold me," she whispered shakily. "Grey, I ache so!"

His arms obliged her, crushing with mingled frustration and irritation. His head bent over her and he rocked her against his big body until they both calmed, until their stormy pulses began to throb normally. The voices were close, now.

All of a sudden, his chest began to shake against her as laughter rumbled up from it. "I can't believe what I meant to do," he burst out, chuckling. "My God, right in the middle of a bridle path that half the riders in the neighborhood use, in broad daylight. . . . You see what you do to me? I touch you and my common sense goes on vacation."

She laughed, too, glorying in the tight clasp of his arms. It was nice to know she affected him that way, even if it was only desire that caused it.

"Nicky and Collette would have gotten an eyeful,

all right, and we'd never have been able to face your mother again."

He drew away and looked down at her with calm, watchful eyes. "I seem to pick the worst possible times and places to make love to you. In the apartment with Dalton due, in the car, here." He shook his head wistfully. His eyes narrowed, clouded. "Abby, after last night . . . how do you feel about Dalton?"

She started to speak, to tell him that Robert Dalton meant nothing to her now, that she loved Greyson McCallum, that last night had been heaven for her. But she hesitated trying to find the right words, and his face closed up to her. He let her go abruptly as Nick and Collette rode into view a few yards away.

"Isn't it a great morning for a ride?" Nicky laughed, his dry gaze going from Abby's flushed face to McCallum's hard one. "Did we interrupt something?"

"Nothing that didn't need interrupting," McCallum said coolly.

Abby felt a sudden emptiness at the curtness in his tone, but she disguised it with a smile. "Hi, Collette," she said, "I wish I looked that good in jodphurs and a hacking jacket." The young French woman smiled shyly at that.

"You don't look all that bad in my jeans and sweater," Nick teased with a broad wink. "Talk about a good fit . . ."

"When you get your ideas together on that campaign," McCallum told his brother, "give me a call and I'll arrange a meeting with Dalton. Abby and I have to get to the office."

"Sure, Grey. See you, Abby," he added.

McCallum, taciturn and unapproachable, helped Abby mount before he threw his leg over his own horse's back and led the way to the house.

McCallum lit a cigarette, ignoring Abby, once they were on the way to the city again.

"What have I done?" she asked quietly when she couldn't stand his silence a minute longer.

He cocked an eyebrow at her. "What could you have done?" He laughed shortly.

"You're so quiet . . ." she murmured.

He took a draw from the cigarette and blew it out, controlling the powerful sports car with the same deft hands he'd used to control Abby last night. "I'm working out that White case in my mind, honey," he said after a minute.

"Are you sure?" Her eyes were more revealing than she knew, wide and green and faintly apprehensive as they met his across the short distance that separated them.

"I'm sure." He winked at her, and she relaxed a little. She settled down in her seat with a long sigh. Everything would be all right, now.

The morning was hectic, and Abby felt as if she were being torn in two by the pressure of clients and a phone that wouldn't stop ringing, and by McCallum's growing impatience.

She eased into his office with a file he'd demanded ten minutes earlier, to find him glaring down at a scatter of notes and documents on his desk. His jacket was off, his tie loosened, his sleeves rolled up over muscular tanned forearms sprinkled with dark hairs. Abby stood there for a long minute just looking at the broad, hard face she'd begun to love so dearly.

He looked up, anger glittering in his unblinking silver gaze. "I asked for that over fifteen minutes ago," he said shortly.

"And you'd have gotten it if the phone hadn't decided to ring off the hook, and that woman whose divorce you handled for a favor hadn't called to wail out her problems to me, and Jerry hadn't asked for the file on his divorce case . . ."

"I don't pay you for excuses," he replied.

He hadn't spoken to her that way since she started to work for him. Perhaps the rough morning had made her sensitive, or their delicate new relationship had left her unprepared for such a flat statement to remind her of her real status in his life. Whatever the reason, tears began to slip hotly down her cheeks.

"Abby!" He threw down the pencil he was jotting notes with and went around the desk.

She tried to back away, but his arms caught her and brought her close to his big, warm body.

"No, don't fight me," he said in a tone that was

worlds away from the sharp, hurting one he'd used seconds before.

"I don't understand you," she managed brokenly. She leaned her sodden cheek against his shirt and sighed.

"I don't understand myself when it comes to you," he admitted dryly. He folded her closer, until she felt as if they were joined, every inch of the way, up and down. "Oh, Abby, it's been a rough morning, hasn't it?" he murmured as he rocked her gently back and forth. "I haven't snapped at you in a long time."

"Not since yesterday," she agreed. A smile peeked through the tears.

He tilted her wet face up to his soft, amused eyes. "You ought to be used to it by now."

"I am. It just stings more than it used to," she said without meaning to.

His long forefinger traced the curve where her lips parted over her pearly teeth. "Does it?" he asked.

She went very still in his arms, amazed at the sensations he could arouse so easily. Only his finger touched her, but she felt the reaction all the way to her toes.

"No one ever affected me the way you do," she said shakily.

He was breathing a little harder, a little faster. "How?"

She caught his free hand and pressed it to the underside of her soft breast, holding it there while she looked up into his eyes.

"Like this," she whispered. "Feel it?"

"Very soft," he whispered back, smiling as his hand took the delicate weight and molded it gently.

"I meant my heartbeat," she murmured unsteadily.

"I'd rather touch your breast," he whispered, bending. He brushed his mouth over hers slowly, tenderly. "I held you naked in my arms," he breathed, as if he could hardly believe it, "yet this morning you look almost virginal. Are you the same woman who sank her teeth into my shoulder and begged me not to stop?"

She reached up and linked her arms behind his head, going on tiptoe to keep the devastating contact with his teasing mouth. "I never knew it could be that way with a man," she said softly. "It was so beautiful, Grey."

He drew back for an instant and scowled at her. His silver eyes narrowed as he studied her worshipping eyes. "Abby, you're not getting involved, are you?"

She blinked. "Involved?"

"Emotionally." His eyes cut into hers like silver knives. His hands moved up to frame her face and hold it steady under the unblinking appraisal. "Are you?"

She closed her eyes in self-defense. She knew how he felt about that. If she admitted what she was beginning to feel, he'd walk away forever, and she knew that, too.

She laughed nervously. "Do we have to analyze it?" she asked, averting her eyes so that she missed the expression that crossed his face like a shadow.

"No," he said after a minute. "We don't have to analyze it. Kiss me, Abby," he whispered against her mouth. He half lifted her against his powerful body. "Kiss me hard, baby . . ."

Her nails bit into the nape of his neck as she obeyed him, her mouth opening to his, her tongue touching his, answering its gentle, slow thrust, her thighs lifting, trembling against his. A soft, hungry moan sobbed out of her as he deepened the kiss, his mouth expert, demanding, blotting out everything except the need that flared up like a torch between them.

He let her slide back to the floor, his eyes watching her steadily. "Tonight," he said deeply, "when we get back to the apartment, I'm going to undress you inch by aching inch. I'm going to carry you into my bedroom and kiss you all the way down to your toes before I take you."

The words, and the intensity with which he said them, made her tremble. "McDougal . . ." she reminded him breathlessly.

A corner of his mouth went up wickedly. "It's her day off, Abby," he whispered. "There won't be anyone to see us, or to interrupt us. And this time . . ." The nagging buzz of the intercom broke the spell violently. McCallum released Abby with a muttered curse and went to jab his finger at the switch.

"Well?" he growled.

"Uh, Mr. McCallum, it's Mr. Dalton for you on line one," Jan said nervously.

"Tell him I'll only be a minute," he said, cutting off the connection without waiting for a reply. His eyes met Abby's apologetically. "Lunch in twenty minutes, honey," he said with a smile.

She nodded, her eyes full of dreams. She went out and closed the door behind her.

But when lunchtime came, McCallum shot through the door of his office like a cyclone, jerking on his suit coat as he came, his face like a thundercloud. He was on the heels of a frantic telephone call Abby had just put through.

"I'll be at the jail," he told Abby curtly. "White just tried to hang himself." And he was gone.

She barely heard Jan coming down the hall. Surely after all the work they'd done trying to prove that Wilfred White was innocent, he wasn't going to die before it even got to trial?

"Trouble?" Jan asked.

"Big trouble. Wilfred White just tried to hang himself," Abby told her. "Mr. McCallum's on his way to the jail."

"Mr. McCallum?" Jan teased. "Your lipstick's smeared, did you know? Too bad about White," she added with a grimace. "You've put in a lot of time with the boss on this one. That suicide attempt will look bad, too; like an admission of guilt."

"McCallum will find some way to use it to his advantage," Abby said from experience. "You just wait and see."

"It wouldn't surprise me," Jan agreed. "Want to go to lunch with me? I'm not tall and ruggedly handsome and magnificent in court, but I'll buy you a hamburger, just the same."

Abby laughed. "You're on, and after this morning, I won't mind at all if you aren't magnificent in court. It will probably mean that you don't have such a low boiling point!"

McCallum came back two hours later, looking every bit as ill-tempered as he had when he left. "Damned fool," he bit off on the way into his office. "Three days before the trial begins, and he has to do a Greek tragedy in the damned jail!"

"Will it go against him that much?" Abby asked.

"That's a question for the clergy," he snapped. "He's dead."

He went into his office and slammed the door. Abby stared after him. McCallum had grown genuinely fond of the eighteen-year-old boy who was accused of murdering a liquor store owner in the course of a robbery attempt. White had been intelligent and pleasant, not at all the kind of man who'd murder someone. White had seemed rather reserved to her, a gentle sort of person. Of course, the complaint stated that he'd allegedly been on drugs when he went into the liquor store to rob it.

McCallum had put in a lot of hours on the preparation. He thought the boy was innocent, and he was determined to free him. Abby smiled wistfully. He was like that about his clients. He never took a case unless he believed in his client's innocence. And he very rarely lost one. This particular one was going to hurt more than most. White had a wife, a wispy little thing who was five months pregnant.

She left her desk and went into McCallum's office. He was sitting in his big padded chair facing the window, a forgotten cigarette in his hand, his jacket off, his big body faintly slumped as if he were exhausted. He probably was, and hurt, to boot. He could be very human at times, despite that rough exterior. He cared deeply about people, despite his maintained emotional distance from his women.

Abby went around the desk and stood beside him, hesitation keeping the words on her tongue.

He reached out a big hand and caught hers, just holding it while he smoked. "His wife lost the baby this morning," he said blankly. "He was depressed over that, and one of the other prisoners started taunting him about what it was going to be like when they shut him up in a federal prison for the rest of his life." He drew a deep, slow breath. "He was an outdoorsman, you know, he hated closed places. I should have spent more time with him," he ground out, jerking his eyes up to Abby's. "I should have convinced him that we'd win the case."

There was anguish in his eyes, his face. "Grey, all

we can do is our best," she said gently. "And you did that. You can't live people's lives for them."

"Is that going to comfort his widow?" he asked curtly.

"No. But I thought it might comfort you," she said gently. "It hurts very badly, doesn't it?"

He drew a sharp breath and pressed her hand. "Yes, Abby. It hurts."

She reached down and gently took the cigarette from the dark hand, crushing it out in the ashtray. Then she eased down into his lap and her fingers smoothed the cool, black hair away from his forehead. Once, she'd never have dared such an intimacy, but it seemed to come naturally now. She bent and kissed him softly, slowly, his forehead, his thick, dark eyebrows, his closed eyelids, his cheeks, his chiseled lips, his chin . . . she kissed him as if they were both children, lost and hurt and afraid. And he seemed to sense it, because he began to kiss her back the same way, with a tenderness that took her breath.

His hands cupped her face and he looked down at her with darkening eyes. "Abby," he breathed softly. Nothing more, just her name, but the way he said it made her think of an open field of wild flowers, of the wind breaking the treetops.

"Let's go home, Grey," she said gently. "And I'll make you forget it."

He sighed roughly and leaned his forehead against hers. "I'd give five years of my life to do that, to lie down with you and give each other the pleasure we did last night. But I can't, Abby. Dalton's on his way here, and he's having dinner with us tonight as well. I've got to get this merger out of the way."

She swallowed down her hurt pride. "Oh. I see."

"No, you don't," he said enigmatically. His eyes searched hers. "You never have. But one of these days, Miss Summer, you may take off your dark glasses and see the world."

She studied his tie. "Did you have to invite him for dinner?" she asked.

She felt his powerful thighs stiffen under her, felt the minute contraction of his arms. "No. But I thought it might be a good idea at this point."

Her eyes darted back up to his. "I don't understand."

"What an understatement." He was wearing his poker face now, nothing showed under it. "Hadn't you better get back to your desk?"

"Most employers would give a lot to have me sit on their laps," she informed him, sitting up straight.

"I'll amen that," he agreed. One big hand slid under the hem of her skirt and up her smooth, lovely thigh, while his eyes traced an appreciative path behind it. "God, I've never seen legs like these before. Long and silky and sexy as hell." He drew her back down against him and kissed her, his mouth hard and hungry, holding the kiss until she moaned and clung to him. He drew back a whisper. "I've got to be sure, Abby, and so have you," he murmured. "It won't hurt either one of us to wait a few more days."

"That wasn't what you said this morning," she managed through lips that still stung from his kiss.

He scowled. "That was before . . . never mind. Up you go, you sexy creature. We've got work to do."

"Slave driver," she muttered, getting to her feet. She smoothed down her skirt and smiled at him. "Feel better?"

"I ache to the soles of my shoes, if you call that feeling better," he said with dry humor.

"Not my fault, counselor, I offered to do something about it," she reminded him with a demure smile.

He leaned back with a hard sigh. "I want you very badly, Miss Summer," he said bluntly. "But until I get a few things straight in my mind, I think we'd better keep this at a manageable level."

That didn't make sense at all, but she wasn't clear-minded enough at the moment to puzzle it out.

"Whatever you want, Grey," she murmured on her way out.

"Not quite," he said under his breath. "Not yet, anyway. Get me Nicky on the phone, honey."

"Of course."

"What did we interrupt this morning?" Nick asked when Abby reached him, and she could see the wicked grin on his face in her mind.

"Not a thing," she protested.

"Sure," he laughed, "that was why you had pine straw all down your back and Grey was ready to throw a punch at me."

"I fell," she lied through a wistful smile. "And Grey is always grumpy early in the morning."

"You ought to know," Nicky said.

"Anyway," she continued, "your big brother wants to speak to you. Hold on a minute."

She pressed the right button, buzzed McCallum, and then waited for him to answer before she put the receiver down. She hadn't heard the office door open, and her back had been to it. When Robert Dalton suddenly appeared in the threshold, she felt a jolt of surprise.

"Oh, you startled me!" she burst out, breathless.

"I'd like to do a lot more than that, Abby," he teased. "Are you all right?"

She stood up, trying to catch her breath. "I'm not usually this jumpy," she murmured.

He moved closer and caught her by the waist. His smile was full of memories. "You were once. That first time I kissed you, remember? In my office at the shipyards, with workers going back and forth outside the window, and I thought there'd never been anything as sweet as your mouth."

Involuntarily, her eyes went to his lips as she recalled that long ago day, and the wonder of finding someone to care about who seemed to care as much about her. She smiled wistfully.

"So you do remember," Dalton breathed as he bent and kissed her softly, gently, a salute to something that had passed like a faint sun shadow on the meadow.

She didn't fight him, but her hands went to push gently at his chest—just as the door opened and McCallum came out of the office.

Abby didn't even have to ask what he was thinking. It was obvious. He scowled at both of them, and the look he gave Abby made her want to wither.

She opened her mouth to speak, but Dalton beat her to it. "Reminiscing, Grey," he murmured with a glint in his eyes. "That's all, we were just . . . reminiscing."

But that wasn't how it sounded, and Abby began to wonder if his apparent surrender to her suggestion that they close the door on the past had been sincere. It looked very much as if he was trying to show McCallum that he was still the man in possession, despite Abby's residence with the younger man.

"If you'll come in, we'll get started," McCallum told him in a cold tone. "Nick will be here in about fifteen minutes. Abby, get us some coffee."

She glared after him, refusing to give him the satisfaction of an argument. Unless she missed her guess, he was going to be spoiling for a fight when they got back to his apartment. She knew that look of his very well.

She took them the coffee, holding back a scathing

comment about not being the maid before she swept back out again. It was her break, and she sat down with her legal pad, to jot down a fiery argument that said absolutely nothing, but relieved her frustration. Why hadn't she said something? Why hadn't she come right out and told McCallum that Dalton wasn't part of her future?

"Idiot," she muttered.

"Someone call?" Nicky asked from behind her.

"They're both in there," she said, gesturing toward McCallum's door. "Want me to announce you?"

He shook his head, sauntering past her to open the door. "Never give Grey any warning, it's suicide."

She muffled a giggle when the door closed behind him.

It took a little over an hour for the conference to break up, during which the phone seemed to have a nervous breakdown. Abby did little else but answer it and explain why Mr. McCallum couldn't come to the phone right then. It was a relief when the office door opened and the three men came through it.

"We'll meet you at the Rendezvous Lounge at seven," McCallum told Robert Dalton.

"I'll be there. See you later, Abby," Dalton added and paused by her long enough to drop a kiss on her forehead. She stared after him, stunned by the gesture.

"I'll say good-bye, too; I left a client sitting in my

office," Nicky murmured. "See you both later."

But neither of them answered him. Abby and McCallum faced each other like championship contenders, wary and taut, while the silence stretched like a Texas highway between them.

CHAPTER NINE

"I vaguely remember telling you that I don't enjoy being made to look like a fool," McCallum told her in his courtroom voice.

She straightened. "And might I ask why you think you do?"

"What the hell kind of games are you playing, Abby?" he growled. "What, exactly, is the relationship between you and 'Grandad'?"

"He's only four years older than you, o ancient one!" she shot back.

"The whole idea of moving in with me was supposed to be keeping him at bay," he reminded her.

"That was when I thought he'd be a threat," she said. "He isn't."

"Of course not. You want him and he wants you.

And now that he's separated, the path is clear, isn't it?" He smiled, a cold smile that hurt her.

She started to tell him that it wasn't true, that he was the only man she wanted, or loved. He obviously didn't feel the same way, with all his warnings about getting "involved." Her pride froze the words in her throat. She couldn't tell him how she really felt.

While she was hesitating, he went back into his office and closed the door.

He didn't speak to her again until they were back in his apartment. They'd both dressed for the evening, McCallum in his dark suit and tie, Abby in a vivid red gown with a handkerchief hem, a nipped waist, and a very low neckline.

"How appropriate," he murmured, casting her a cool glance.

She stiffened. "The color?" she asked, with an overly sweet smile. "Yes, isn't it? I thought I might open a brothel someday and this is just the dress to drum up business."

"You said it, honey, I didn't," he growled. "It's five thirty. We'd better be going."

She followed him to the door with an emptiness in her that she'd never expected. Her fingers touched his sleeve lightly, and his big body went taut at the action.

"Let's not argue," she pleaded gently.

His face was still like a block of ice, but he did smile—if it could be called that. "Why not? By all means, let's be civilized. I assume you'll be moving out in the near future?" he added with chilling politeness. "After all, there's hardly any reason left for you to stay, is there?" And he opened the door.

She thought about it all the way to the exclusive downtown restaurant, and by the time they were escorted to Robert Dalton's table, she was in a state of depression that was trancelike. She'd gotten so used to being with McCallum. Having breakfast with him, watching television with him, talking and laughing and making love with him, and how was she going to get used to the idea of being alone again? How was she going to cope with life without McCallum?

Her hungry eyes fastened on his profile as they wound through the tables, drinking in every line of his dark, broad face. He was the most elegant man she'd ever known, and by far the most masculine. He attracted female eyes without even trying; especially Abby's. She studied his mouth and remembered the way it felt hard against hers. Her eyes slid down the big, hard-muscled frame and she could still feel its warmth and weight in that bed at his mother's house as he taught her all the secret pleasures of lovemaking.

He heard the tiny little sigh and glanced down at her. "Impatient?" he chided coolly.

She wondered miserably what he'd have done if she'd admitted that it was the memory of his ardent lovemaking the night before that had prompted the sound?

"Yes, of course," she replied with practiced unconcern. She didn't look at him again.

Robert Dalton rose as they approached the table. "Good evening," he said formally, smiling at McCallum and treating Abby to a long, appreciative look. "Abby, you look enchanting in that dress."

"I've been told that the color suits me," she murmured as he seated her.

"It does," Dalton murmured. "It's bright and vivid and eye-catching—like you."

"Why, Robert, how very gallant," she sighed. Her angry eyes met McCallum's across the table.

But the taciturn attorney ignored the dig and concentrated on his menu. "What will you have, Abby?" he asked with icy politeness.

She turned her attention to the tempting dishes, and once McCallum had ordered, he dragged Dalton into a discussion about the merger that lasted all the way through the main course of rack of lamb and didn't end until the lemon mousse was being served. It almost seemed to be deliberate, as if McCallum intended to make it impossible for Dalton to say anything to Abby. However, over the dessert, the older man toyed with the long stem of his wineglass. He smiled at Abby and leaned toward her.

"We had lemon mousse that first evening we spent together," he said in a soft, gentle tone. "Remember?"

She smiled back. "It was at the restaurant on the top of the skyscraper," she recalled. "And I wore a business suit while all the other women were dressed in silk and covered with jewelry. I wanted to go through the floor."

He laughed delightedly. "I thought you were the most striking woman there," he reminded her.

"And you were surely the most striking man," she replied with a glance toward McCallum, who was glowering down into his wineglass. She averted her gaze with a secret smile. "We had fun together."

McCallum set the wineglass down with a thud that all but shook the table. "If you two are finished, I've got a brief to work on tonight. I need to get home. Coming, Abby?"

"I'll bring you home if you'd like," Dalton said quickly, his eyes hopeful. "We could go dancing," he added.

Abby smiled demurely. "Why, thank you, Robert, I'd like that."

McCallum shook hands with Dalton and went to pay the check. He left the restaurant without another glance in Abby's direction. Good enough for him, she thought bitterly. The way he'd been behaving, it was a relief not to have to be around him. She told herself that, but his treatment of her had hurt just the same. He'd as well as told her to leave the apartment, to get out of his life. She supposed that he was afraid of any further involvement with her, and that was why he wanted her to leave. But it didn't seem possible that he could care so little after their night together, when he'd been as tender a lover as any woman could want. Surely a man couldn't be that loving unless he loved . . . except in McCallum's case, she added silently. He was just an experienced man and she'd been a challenge with her coolness, her poise. He'd wanted to prove that he could get under her guard and he'd done that. How he'd done that!

"I said," Dalton murmured gently, "how would you like to try that new lounge down the street? It's a disco, but I think we can manage to blend in."

She smiled at him halfheartedly. "I'd like that very much. Shall we go?"

The disco was bright and colorful and loud, and Abby drank far more than she should have. She danced uninhibitedly, light on her feet, and closed her eyes as the throbbing music and lights washed her in a loud oblivion. She wasn't drunk when Dalton gently suggested that it was time to leave. But she was on the verge.

"I feel a little fuzzy," she admitted when Dalton pulled up at McCallum's apartment building. "Nice, but blurred around the edges."

Dalton sighed. "Oh, Abby, I had such hopes for tonight," he murmured. "I told Grey that we were . . . well, that's not important now. You've had him on your mind all night, haven't you? I have to admit that at first I thought you were using him as a cover, to keep me from getting too close. But that's not so, is it? You really care about him."

Even through the blur of the alcohol, that hit

home. "Yes," she admitted after a minute. "I care—terribly."

"There's no chance for me?"

She looked at him wistfully. "A year ago, yes. But not now. I'm sorry. I truly am."

"Not half as sorry as I am." He leaned forward and kissed her cheek gently. "I should have let well enough alone. You told me it was over, but I didn't believe you. I hope I haven't messed things up too much for you and Grey."

That remark flew right over her swimming head. "Good night, Robert," she murmured. "Thank you for my evening."

"Thank you for mine. Good night, Abby."

She fumbled with her key once she was at the door of the apartment, and she wondered if McCallum was home. She walked in, closing the door behind her, and found the living room dimly lit, the door to his study closed with a sliver of light showing under it. But there wasn't a sound to be heard.

Abby made her way to her room and stripped off the red dress with a silent vow never to wear it again as she hung it back in the closet.

She studied her slip-clad body in the full-length mirror on the closet door with a critical eye. The low-cut neckline of the lacy apricot slip was enticing, as was the raised hem. With her long blond hair cascading around her shoulders, she wasn't bad looking at all.

Her lips smiled lazily. Perhaps McCallum had just

been jealous of Dalton. That would explain his moodiness, his irritability, his treatment of her. If that was the case, then all she had to do was go and seduce him and everything would be all right. She wouldn't have to leave, they'd live happily ever after, and Dorothy would indeed get back to Kansas.

It made so much sense that she didn't think any further than that. She opened her door and went across the hall to McCallum's bedroom. But the bed was still made, and the coverlet untouched. He must be in the study.

She wobbled down the hall, convinced that she wasn't even tipsy. She simply felt capable of conquering the world, that was all. And if she could do that, conquering McCallum shouldn't present too large a problem.

Sure enough, Grey was sitting behind his desk. His shirt was open down the front, his sleeves rolled back. His dark hair was mussed and his face showed every hard line. He looked up at her entrance with eyes so cold they made her shiver.

"Still up?" she teased. She leaned back against the closed door for support. "I thought you'd be in bed by now."

"Thought, or hoped?" he asked carelessly. "I hope you didn't get the idea that I was waiting up for you. I couldn't care less how late you come in."

"Of course not." She smiled woozily. "Jealous, Grey?"

He cocked an eyebrow and laid down his fountain pen. "Of you?"

"You've been furious at me since I went out with Robert the first time," she reminded him.

"Good God, of course I have!" he burst out. "I didn't expect to have you hanging on his sleeve the whole time he was in town. Damn it, hasn't it occurred to you that I'm trying to conduct a million-dollar business deal with him? How in hell can I get his attention when he's lavishing it on you?"

She blinked. "Oh, come on, now," she laughed. "Is that the truth?"

He stood up and came around the desk. "You're drunk," he said with faint contempt.

"I only had four," she muttered.

"Four what? Double Scotches? That's what you look like."

"Do you like the way I look, Grey?" she murmured, moving close. She lifted her hands and slid them inside his unfastened shirt, tangling them in the thick growth of hair over the smooth, hard muscles of his chest and stomach. She went on tiptoe to press her lips slowly, hungrily against his. But there was no response. None at all.

She drew back and frowned up at him. She couldn't read a trace of emotion in those rigid features.

But she wasn't giving up. Not now. With a tiny smile she slid the straps of her thin slip off her shoulders and let it fall to the floor. She stood there, nude except for her panties, and watched his eyes trace a path down the length of her and up again, lingering on the high swell of her breasts before they levered back up to meet her eyes. The look on his face made her want to cringe. It wasn't desire. It was a kind of contempt that got through the alcoholic haze and made her sick.

"I don't need any leftovers, Abby," he said coolly.

Shocked, humiliated, she pulled the slip back on with a jerky motion, her face hot and red with embarrassment.

"I . . . after the . . . after last night, I thought . . ." she stammered.

"Did you pretend that I was Dalton, Abby?" he asked carelessly, bending his ruffled head to light a cigarette. His silver eyes pinned hers. "Was that why you were so loving in my arms? Didn't Dalton ask you to help 'keep me satisfied' until this deal was closed?"

"No!" she burst out.

He laughed shortly and turned away. "Perhaps not. But you're not going to use me to bring him to heel. Pack your things, Abby. You're leaving here in the morning. You can move in with Dalton or follow him back to Charleston. And furthermore, I think it would be in the best interests of both of us if you started looking for another job. I'll expect you to work for at least two weeks, but I'll find a replacement within a couple of days."

She gaped at him. Tears welled behind her eyes. "I

wasn't using you!" she cried. "Grey, I don't want Robert Dalton anymore, I don't!"

He spared her a glance as he slid down into his desk chair. "Strange, that isn't what he told me."

So that explained Dalton's strange remark out in the car, the one that had gone over her head. And McCallum sat there as unyielding as a boulder, his eyes accusing as they met hers. He wasn't prepared to believe anything she said. He was convinced that she was still in love with Dalton, and that was the end of it. He didn't want her.

She turned, her posture drooping, and reached for the doorknob. "I'll take the morning off, if you don't mind," she said proudly. "That will give me enough time to get moved and put in my application at an employment agency."

There was a brief hesitation before he spoke. "I suppose I can spare you."

"Jan's roommate is looking for a job," she mentioned, recalling Jan's enthusiastic efforts in her friend's behalf. "You might ask her."

"Abby . . ."

She bit her lip to keep from crying. She couldn't look at him. "You're right, it's for the best. Damn you, Greyson McCallum, I wish I never had to see you again!" She opened the door and ran all the way to her room.

He was already gone when she went in to breakfast, and it was a blessed relief. Abby hadn't known how she was going to face him after her exhibition last night. Just the memory of it made her face flame with self contempt. How could she have been so brazen, so blatant? She'd never forgive herself. She should have left well enough alone and gone to bed. As it was, she didn't know how she was ever going to be able to look him in the eye. She didn't want to, she told herself. She'd meant it when she told him she didn't want to see him again. But that wasn't going to be possible. She was going to have to work those two weeks, and she couldn't imagine a purer torment.

How simple everything had seemed when McCallum had suggested that she move in with him. How uncomplicated. Abby had never expected it to wind up in such a tangle.

"Have enough?" Mrs. McDougal asked from the doorway with a smile.

"Plenty, thank you, it was delicious," Abby said automatically, while she felt as if she'd eaten cardboard.

"Then I'll see you this evening. Have a nice day," the housekeeper said pleasantly, as she turned back into the kitchen.

Abby could have cried. No, Mrs. McDougal wouldn't see her, not that evening or any other. She wondered if Vinnie Nichols would move in with McCallum now. It seemed likely. She got up from the table, leaving a full cup of coffee untouched.

* * *

Her apartment seemed alien now. She missed the big easy chair she'd curled up in while she was staying with McCallum. She missed hearing his voice, his step. She even missed his temper. Life was going to be so lonely now.

She took her time about unpacking, while mentally she thought through her options. She could go back to reporting, of course. She had enough experience to qualify for a copyeditor's job. Or she could find another legal firm to work for. She still had high hopes for the novel she was working on, but that was going to take more time than she had. She couldn't expect to just pop it in the mail and have a check back in two weeks. She was more likely to have a rejection slip in that length of time. First novels were notoriously hard to market, and she had no mistaken ideas that she was a phenomenal talent. The competition was fierce, and Abby was a beginner. Someday, she fully expected to break into the market, but she was realistic enough to know that it would take some effort, as well as time.

The immediate thing was to look for another job. She tidied up her apartment and went downtown to the state employment agency. Unemployment was rampant and she had to wait for a long time to see a counselor. But it didn't take a great deal of time to fill out the form and answer the questions.

"You're in luck," the young woman behind the desk told her with a smile. "We've got an attorney looking for a secretary. He's just passed his bar exam and it'll be a one-girl office. Want to try?"

"Oh, yes!" Abby said gratefully.

She was given a name and address and she beat a path to the nearby office building where Elton Pettigrew, Attorney at Law, had just opened his practice.

He was a personable young man with blond hair and green eyes, and he was impressed with Abby's secretarial skills.

"There's only one thing," she said nervously. "I'd just as soon you didn't say anything to my previous employer about my working here. There was a . . . a personal problem there."

Pettigrew's eyebrows levered up. "McCallum, huh?" he asked with a knowing smile. "I don't know him personally, but I hear he's quite a success with women. Most women," he amended. "Did he make a pass, if you don't mind my asking?"

She looked down at her skirt. "I lived with him," she murmured.

"Oh." He shifted uncomfortably. "Sorry. Of course I won't say anything. It isn't necessary, anyway. When can you start, Abby?" he asked with a smile. He indicated the piled-up desk. "I'm pretty desperate."

Abby's mind was whirling. Did she dare? McCallum would be furious. Jan would inherit all her work until a replacement could be found. But what was she worrying about? There were temporary agencies, weren't there? Surely one of them could fill in until McCallum got a new secretary. She'd call Jan, swear her to secrecy and apologize. She brightened. She wouldn't have to endure two weeks of watching McCallum in the office and aching for him at home.

"Today," she said firmly. "I can start right now, if you like."

"You angel!" he laughed. "All right, Miss Summer, sit down and let's get cracking. And I swear on my honor McCallum will never hear your whereabouts from me."

Pettigrew was an angel himself, to work for. He didn't yell, lose his temper, or throw things. He was considerate, kind, and pleasant—all the things McCallum would never be. It was a pity that Abby had learned to love him, disagreeable traits and all. She felt like a widow away from her volatile boss.

She left an hour early with another new idea in mind. She found an apartment practically next door to Pettigrew's office and paid two weeks' rent in advance. Then she rushed to her own apartment which was, fortunately, a furnished one, packed all her things—again—and moved out. By midnight, she had everything arranged, and all the doors were closed on the past.

She'd forgotten to call Jan. She did that the minute the unpacking was through.

"Were you in bed?" Abby asked when Jan answered drowsily.

"Abby! Where are you, how are you, what—" she began frantically.

"I'm fine," she said gently. "I just got a new job and I'm . . . I'm not in the city anymore," she lied, hating the necessity of it. "I'm so sorry, Jan, but McCallum and I had a horrible argument, and I just couldn't bear another minute of him. I know you've got more than you can handle . . ."

"I got an agency girl, don't worry about that," she muttered. "I'm worried about *you.* Honest to God, Abby, McCallum's been like a wild man today. He called hospitals and even the morgue. Please, let me tell him that you're all right, at least!"

Guilt, she thought miserably. He was remembering what he'd said last night and feeling miserable because he thought something had happened to her.

"Tell him," she said carelessly, "but I'm not going to tell even you where I am or what I'm doing. Jan, I never want to see him again. Never."

"What did he do?" Jan groaned. "Abby . . ."

"It's all in the past," came the weary reply. "I'm so tired, Jan. I'd just had all I could take. McCallum told me last night to get out of the apartment and find another job. Well, I did both, and I don't know what he's upset about. He told me to go."

"I don't think he meant to, is the thing," Jan sighed. "Men do strange things when they're in love and jealous."

"Want to hear the truth?" Abby asked. "McCallum let me stay in the apartment to protect me from getting involved with Robert Dalton. I . . . I knew him from Charleston, you remember."

"I remember. You were in a bad way," Jan said gently.

"I'm in a worse one now," Abby laughed miserably. "Anyway, there was never any real emotion on McCallum's part, he just wanted to keep me on the job. I'd told him I'd quit if I had to see Robert every day."

"And he let you move in just because of that?" Jan asked slyly. "Uh-uh," she murmured. "Not McCallum. He never does anything without a motive. Even Vinnie Nichols has never stayed more than a night at his apartment, did you know that? I found it out accidentally, and it quite shocked me. He values his privacy more than anything else in life. He wouldn't share it just as a favor."

"So I thought, too, once," Abby said, recalling with painful clarity the offer she'd made McCallum as she shed her slip—an offer he'd refused coldly and contemptuously. "But I was wrong. And so are you, my friend."

"Abby, did Nick ever tell you what McCallum said at the Christmas party? He said he was going to when I talked with him a couple of days ago. Did he ever?"

Abby frowned. "No."

"McCallum told Nick that he'd have given half his practice to kiss you under the mistletoe, but he was afraid that if he did you'd quit, and he'd never have another chance to get close to you."

Abby felt her heart spin around. She drew a

steadying breath. Well, McCallum had gotten close all right, she thought. The problem was, he'd discovered that he didn't like being close to Abby, physically or otherwise. That's why he'd sent her away.

"Did you hear me?" Jan prompted.

"I heard you. But it doesn't matter. Not now."

"Do you love him, Abby?" Jan asked bluntly.

She bit her lip. "Oh, Jan, I do love him so," she whispered. "I tried not to, and leaving him . . ." She swallowed tears. "It was the hardest thing I've ever done. But he doesn't want me, he sent me away, he hates me . . . !"

"You're upset. It's my fault, I'm sorry." There was a pause. "Will you do something for me? There's a file at the office that you've written a note about, and I can't make it out—it's on that murder trial coming up, the Harris case—could I call you about ten in the morning? McCallum will be out," she added, "and you can decipher the note and tell me what to do with the things in your desk, where to forward your mail . . ."

Abby sniffed back the tears. "Okay. I'll give you the number, but you swear that you won't give it to McCallum."

"All right, I swear," Jan said reluctantly. "Talk to you in the morning then. Good night, Jan."

"Good night, Abby," came the reply. Now why did Jan sound so satisfied? Well, she could tell McCallum to stop worrying, anyway, but he wouldn't know where Abby was. Not a chance.

* * *

Abby had a fresh cup of coffee in front of her as she rifled through the papers on her desk. Pettigrew had gone to court, and the office was empty. She'd caught up the correspondence and was working on a divorce petition. It looked like a slow day, so she didn't feel guilty about taking the time to have a second cup of coffee.

The phone rang four times before Abby picked it up breathlessly and gave the name of the law firm.

"Hi, Abby," Jan said with a smile in her voice. "Are you still okay?" she added gently.

"Fine. Just fine. Now read me that note."

"I'll get it right now." There was a long, long pause before Jan came back on the line. "Okay, here it is. Something about calling up Newman . . ."

"But that was about a case we finished weeks ago," Abby protested. "Are you sure that's the right note?"

"I thought it was . . . yes, that's the only one in the file. Maybe it was misfiled," Jan stammered.

Abby sighed. It wasn't like Jan to get rattled. "As for my stuff in the desk, just put it in a box and keep it by you. There's bound to be a day when McCallum is out of town and that's when I'll come by to get it."

"I'll do that. You take care of yourself, hear?"

"I will. You, too, my friend. Bye, Jan."

She hung up and stared at the receiver. Tears began to roll down her cheeks. That was that. The last link severed. Now, all she had to do was learn to live without Greyson McCallum.

Thirty minutes later, she was just finishing the petition when she heard the office door open. She whirled around to see who it was, and her heart seemed to levitate and hang in midair.

"Hello, Abby," McCallum said quietly from the doorway.

CHAPTER TEN

She stared at him with tear-filled eyes, and hated the weak part of her that wanted to get up and run to him. But pride and hurt kept her seated.

"How did you find me?" she asked shakily.

He shrugged. "I looked up the address in the telephone directory . . ."

"Jan told you the name of the law firm," she finished for him.

He scowled. "Thank God she did. Do you know I've been all the way to Charleston looking for you? I followed Dalton back there, expecting that I'd find you with him. When he hadn't seen you, I had to assume the worst." He started toward her, his whole stance menacing. The dark brown suit he was wearing made his silver eyes seem even lighter as they glittered down at her. "I called hospitals and funeral homes and the morgue. I called the ambulance service and the police. I gave up at two in the morning and went to bed, and even then I couldn't sleep. When Jan came in this morning and told me you'd called and that you were all right, I damned near got down on my knees to thank God that you weren't lying somewhere dead."

She straightened up from the chair, standing behind it for support. "You don't have to worry, I'm fine. I've got a new job, a new apartment—a new start. I'll be fine."

"No, you won't," he said. He stopped just in front of her, and for once he looked every year of his age. He was absolutely haggard, drawn. "I hurt you. I seem to have done quite a lot of that over the past few days. I came here to ask you if you could forgive me."

Her green eyes widened on his face. She'd never once heard McCallum apologize, not to anyone. It was something he didn't do. But he was apologizing to her, with a humility she'd never expected from him.

She dropped her eyes to the coffee on her desk. "That . . . that part of my life is over," she told him gently. "I won't hold a grudge. You can't help what you feel, anymore than I can."

"Do you hate me, Abby?" he asked roughly.

She shook her head. "I . . . it's just that I'm so

ashamed," she whispered. Her voice broke on the word and she half turned away.

He moved with uncanny speed for a man his size, whirling her around to catch her hard and close in his big arms.

"Ashamed of what?" he ground out. His face was unnervingly close, his pulse as erratic as hers. "Of offering yourself to me that night? I wanted you. Oh, God, I wanted you! But I thought Dalton had turned away from you, and you were looking for a substitute. You were half stoned . . ."

"You said you didn't want me." The words came out on broken sobs, and tears streamed down her cheeks.

He held her closer, tilting her mouth up to meet his. "How could I?" he whispered as his lips slowly, softly, parted her trembling lips. "When all I want in the world, in life, is you?"

His mouth opened against hers, pressing her lips along with it, his tongue tracing first the upper lip, then the lower before it shot into her mouth and took absolute possession. He ground her body into his, moving it silkily in a slow, maddening rhythm that very quickly began to have an unmistakable effect on him.

"Come back to the apartment with me, Abby," he said in a rough whisper over her lips. "I want to show you exactly what I feel for you."

"But . . . but I'm working . . ." she protested weakly.

"Put the phones on hold and lock the door. We'll call him later," he said, his eyes eating her.

She was too weak-kneed to argue. She jotted a note telling Pettigrew she'd had an emergency, locked the door, and followed McCallum without another word of protest.

He'd barely closed the apartment door and locked it after a brief, silent ride, when he drew Abby's body against his and began to kiss her—long, slow, deep kisses that very quickly made her moan.

"I missed you," he whispered huskily. His hands unzipped her dress and slid it down her body; her slip followed. "I never knew a man could miss a woman so much." He unhooked her bra and drew it sensuously down her arms. His eyes worshipped her high, bare breasts in the aching silence that followed, before he bent and took each taut nipple in his mouth, tantalizing, caressing, until her fingers caught the back of his head and her body arched to give him better access.

"Undress me," he whispered.

Her hands slipped off his jacket and worked the buttons of his shirt with feverish impatience. She eased it off and ran her hands slowly, aggressively against his broad chest, savoring the feel of it.

"Hurry," he murmured. His hands were all over her, touching, teasing, making her tremble with pleasure.

She eased off his trousers and bent to help him out

of his shoes and socks. There was only one last garment, and her fingers hesitated only briefly before they tugged at the elastic and drew it down. Following an impulse, her lips traveled from his chest down his flat stomach to his thighs. The reaction she got was completely unexpected. With a harsh, deep groan, he caught her around the waist and eased down onto the thick carpet with her, his hands quickly removing her tiny panties before he covered her body with brief, teasing kisses. She writhed in a torment of pleasure, begging, pleading, until she felt his warm, hard body easing down onto hers.

"Look at me," he ground out as his body slowly merged with hers.

With a gasp, she looked straight up into his eyes, her body involuntarily arching, falling.

"I love you," he said in a voice that trembled with hunger.

"I . . . love you," she managed.

It was the last intelligible sound she made for a long, long time as he led her into an intensity of sensation that even surpassed the first time with him. She thought that no woman alive had ever been loved as tenderly, as fiercely, as completely as he loved her on that cool, silky carpet in the middle of the living room.

She could barely breathe at all when he pulled her beside him and lit a cigarette in what seemed like a lifetime later.

He pulled an ashtray down from the end table and

propped it up on his sweaty chest, easing up against the end of the sofa for a back support.

"You see what you drive me to?" he chuckled breathlessly. "My God, on the carpet!"

She laughed delightedly, nuzzling her face into his throat. "I love you," she whispered. "I love you, I love you . . ."

He reached down and kissed her. His lips were cool and he tasted of smoke and tenderness. "I love you," he whispered back. She'd have known without the words. It was in his eyes, in the way he looked at her, touched her. It had been there for a very long time, and she'd never noticed.

"I've worshipped you from afar for months, Miss Summer," he told her gently. "But you were wearing a suit of armor I couldn't get through. I'll always be grateful to Dalton for finding a chink in it for me."

"There hasn't been anything between us, Grey," she said earnestly. "I told him that I loved you."

"He was trying to cause trouble at first, I think," he agreed, "but eventually I worked it out for myself that he was doing the chasing, not you. Abby, I'd give anything to take back what I said and did to you the night I told you to go."

The pain in his eyes hurt her. She reached up and kissed them tenderly, her fingers caressing his broad face. "You just made up for it, counselor," she said with a loving smile.

"Well, just in case there were any doubts left in your mind," he murmured, and his smile teased her.

"I did plan on making it up to you some more—several times," he added, watching her color delightfully. "Just one thing though, love—I suppose you noticed that I didn't do much protecting."

She looked up into his eyes. "Grey, would it matter terribly if I got pregnant?"

He shook his head. "No, ma'am," he said with a grin. "I think pregnant ladies are sexy as hell. There's just one catch."

"What?" she asked suspiciously. She sat up, unconsciously graceful, like a Venus kneeling on the rug, and his eyes ate her. "A wife you didn't mention? A shady past? A . . ."

"You'll have to marry me," he said.

Her eyes searched his. "I'd like that," she said. "But you don't have to."

"I know. I want to." He finished the cigarette and put it out. "I wanted to six months ago. I never believed in commitment until I met you, honey, but right now all I want is to get you in front of a minister before you change your mind."

"I won't do that," she promised. "But if it's all the same to you, I'd like to put something on before you take me to get the license."

He chuckled, reaching up to her. "Later, baby," he whispered as he lay her down. "I'm not quite through explaining how I feel about you."

She reached up to pull his warm, hair-covered body down against the soft bareness of her own with a worshipful smile.

"Don't let me interrupt you, darling," she whispered against his warm mouth, "but isn't Mrs. McDougal due any minute?"

He poised with his mouth just over hers and checked his watch. "So she is. All right, temptress, come on."

He got up and swung her up in his arms to carry her toward the privacy of his bedroom.

"But, Grey, the clothes . . ." she protested, looking over his broad, bronzed shoulder at the scatter of them on the rug.

He only laughed, the sound deep and pleasant in the silence of the apartment. "It'll be good practice for McDougal," he replied.

"Practice?"

He looked down at her as he carried her into the bedroom. "I have a feeling that this could be habit-forming, honey," he murmured as he closed the door.

There was a muffled laugh behind it, a deep chuckle . . . and then silence. Mrs. McDougal, just opening the apartment door, spotted the clothes, smiled broadly, and made a mental note to put dinner back two hours.

LOOK FOR NEXT MONTH'S
CANDLELIGHT ECSTASY ROMANCES™

114 LOVER FROM THE SEA, *Bonnie Drake*
115 IN THE ARMS OF LOVE, *Alexis Hill*
116 CAUGHT IN THE RAIN, *Shirley Hart*
117 WHEN NEXT WE LOVE, *Heather Graham*
118 TO HAVE AND TO HOLD, *Lori Herter*
119 HEART'S SHADOW, *Prudence Martin*
120 THAT CERTAIN SUMMER, *Emma Bennett*
121 DAWN'S PROMISE, *Jo Calloway*

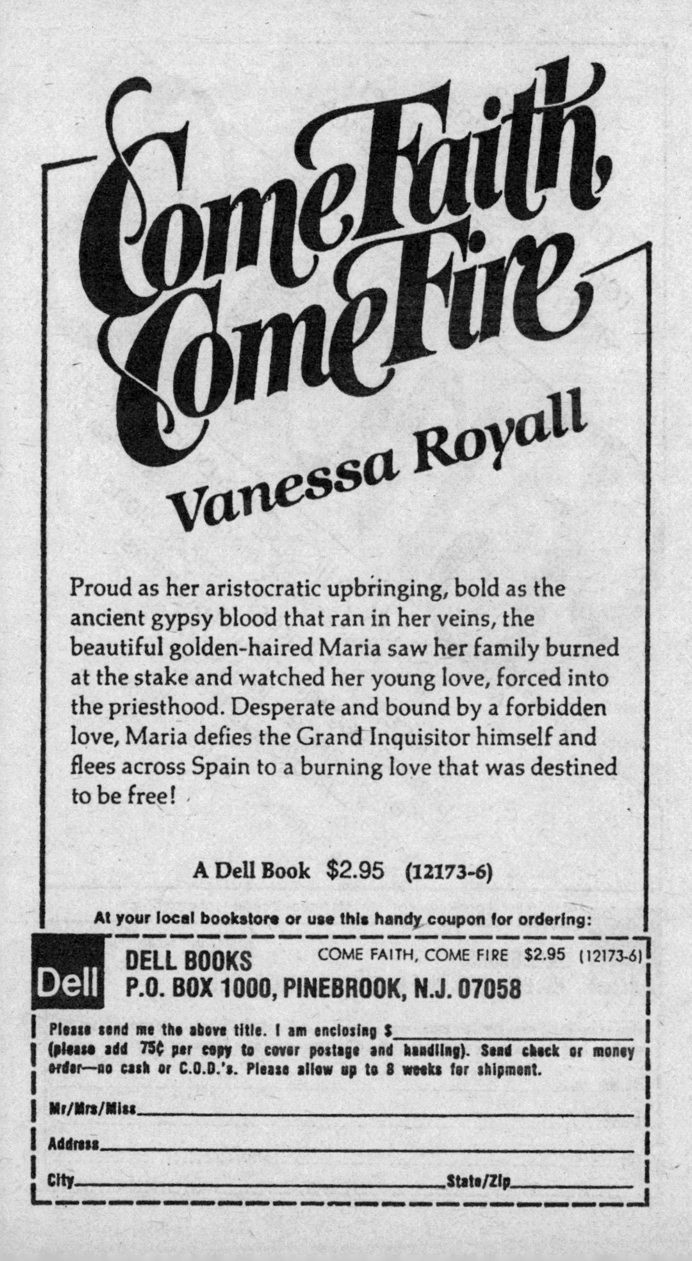